# Secret Behind the Gate

## Zvi A. Sesling

Červená Barva Press
Somerville, Massachusetts

Červená Barva Press
P.O. Box 440357
W. Somerville, MA 02144-3222

www.cervenabarvapress.com

Bookstore: www.thelostbookshelf.com

Cover photo: "silhouette of person walking on road" by Erik Mclean, Pexels

Cover Design: William J. Kelle

ISBN: 978-1-950063-68-0

Library of Congress Control Number: 2023935770

## ACKNOWLEDGMENTS

A number of these stories previously appeared in online and/or hardcopy publications and much appreciation is given to the editors of those publications.

Thank you to Michael C. Keith whose reading of this volume and his book *Let Us Now Speak of Extinction* inspired this book as did Timothy Gager's *Everyday There's Something About Elephants*. And Phil Temples for his reading and suggestions.

A very special thank you to my wife Susan J. Dechter without whose proofreading and editing this book would never have been completed.

# TABLE OF CONTENTS

For Susan

# Secret Behind the Gate

## Freedom Is Not Just Another Word

Pigs are reported to be the smartest of barnyard animals and female pigs smarter than the males. So, it makes sense that a 280-pound sow being transported to the slaughterhouse worked her way out of the back of a trailer transporting it to a future as a platter of bacon or as the ham centerpiece of the family dinner. This sow bobbed and weaved her way through backyards like a star running back, eluding her captors and then the police, who like the Canadian Mounties wanted to prove they could get their man or pig. Finally, the corpulent porker ran out of strength, her legs wobbly, her grunts deeper, just lay down and when roped like a cow she squealed like the pig. She was dragged back to her inevitable fate, learning a lesson rock and roll fans have never learned: freedom is not just another word and there is something left to lose.

## Secret Behind The Gate

The house is lopsided, rotting. All the windows have holes where children throw rocks. Grass grows taller than the children and anyone entering gets an eerie feeling at the gate which guards a cracked cement walkway where a mouse enters followed by a cat. Neither is seen again. At night a strange light inside; during daytime there is a creaking noise. Behind the walls is the secret. Children dare and double-dare each other to enter the house. Only one child takes the challenge and disappears. The others stop the ice cream truck and buy popsicles. Years later when the house is demolished nothing is found inside.

## She Really Remembered Me

At the fiftieth high school reunion they trot out Old Lady Pogash.
I say to her, "I know I am not supposed to ask a lady her age, but how old are you?"
She glares at me and says, "No, you are not supposed to ask, but I am one hundred and two.'
I respond with a straight face, "Not possible. You were 102 when I had you for Senior English."
She points her crooked finger at me and says sternly, "You always were my most obnoxious student."

## A Run Of Bad Luck

"It hasn't been good," Leroy says to his psychiatrist Dr. Mendenhall. "My luck with women has been a bad run. My first wife Cecilia had an itis. In fact she had every itis known to the medical profession and some they didn't know. First, on our honeymoon she got appendicitis. After we were married a year she developed ileitis, then colitis. She then got a terrible case of conjunctivitis. That was followed by osteoarthritis."
Dr. Mendenhall strokes his moustache, "A run of bad luck for the poor woman I would say," the psychiatrist says.
"Ah, but that's not the end of it," Leroy continues. "Next she got diverticulitis and finally vulvovaginitis."
"And that is when you have an affair with Laura?"
"Yes, but it was desperation. I needed some lovin' and I run into my secretary in a lounge. She has just gotten a divorce and is drowning her misery. She takes me back to her place and makes very passionate love to me, but keeps calling me by her ex-husband's name. I help her find a new job."
Dr. Mendenhall says with a scolding tone, "You have not told me about Zoe."
"Well, Zoe is kind of a free spirit and barely out of her teens. She has a couple boyfriends but tells me she'd always wants to have sex with a married man."
"Why did you stop seeing her?"
"One of her boyfriends throws her out the fifth story window of her apartment building."
"And then?"
"There was a string of quick affairs. One has an STD, one runs off with her professor. Another decides she is a lesbian. Then along comes Florence."
"Ah, yes, Florence. An extension of your bad luck?"
"Is she ever," Leroy says. "We are really destined to meet and marry, which we do. We take wonderful vacations and cruises. Problem is Florence loves to eat sweets. Getst diabetes, loses weight but gets cancer and dies."

"Such a pity," Dr. Mendenhall says shaking his head sadly. "But I sense you may have someone else now."

"Shirley," Leroy says. "I start seeing Shirley. But you know she is one of the victims in the mall shooting two days ago."

## The Bride Wears Black

She is in mourning, wears a black gown and veil. Everyone stands when she enters. The groom is in a coffin of black metal. He is outfitted in a black tuxedo, black shirt and tie and black shoes and socks. The priest is in black garb as is the bride's father. Eight pallbearers all in black stand as her father speaks for bride and groom. When the marriage ceremony is over funeral rites are said. A black hearse carries him to a grave with a black headstone and she is taken to a black house.

## The Search Never Ends

To find you I must navigate a maze of back alleys, narrow with centuries of old wooden houses lining cobblestone streets worn down and broken by years of horse hooves and wagons and a sky that cries like the soon-to-be widow who knows her husband is in captivity. The search goes up a pinching of steps, around narrow bends where no taxi can fit, down slippery slopes one can ski without snow. Mice live in the spaces between stones despite children who try to catch them with old pillow cases and peanut butter. I wish for a trail of footprints, orange peels or pistachio shells. But like a ghost you vaporize and I have to follow the foggy memory fading as the sun sets.

## Hearing Aids

Bertrand realizes he is losing his hearing so he goes to Ultimate Ears and undergoes tests. Finally the hearing specialist tells him he needs a pair of Ultimate Ears X-1 hearing aids.

"You'll be able to hear a pin drop in the middle of traffic jam and the cars will not sound overly loud. These are ultimate in hearing aids." The specialist explains a lot of technical data that Bertrand does not understand but fully appreciates the importance of what he is being told.

After paying $8,000 for a pair of Ultimate Ears X-1 and waiting the two weeks for them to arrive by special carrier at his front door, he signs the receipt and immediately fits them to his ears. To his amazement Bertrand can hear things he has not heard for a long time, the refrigerator, door bell, neighbors arguing next door, dogs barking, mice scurrying across the kitchen floor. More amazing, by adjusting the hearing to Level 1 he can hear the past, FDR's declaration of war, Eisenhower's acceptance speech as newly elected president, Roger Maris' 61st homerun. He is astounded by the history he can tune in. Then on a whim he boosts the hearing to Level 8 and hears things yet to come, a president impeached and another assassinated. A spaceship landing on a moon of Jupiter.

Bertrand literally cannot believe his ears. He wants to return them to Ultimate Ears but decides he will figure out how the stock market will do. While fiddling with the setting he hears his minister praying for his departed soul.

## All's Well That Ends Well

Ken meets Becky when she is twenty and he thirty. Now eighteen years later he is making six figures a year. Because they agree not to have children she has a full time job as an advertising copywriter at a top agency. Their sex life, while slowing a bit from their passionate early days, is still active. They do a lot of things together, go to the local college football games in the fall and the minor league baseball games in spring and summer. They go to plays, movies and occasional concerts. Ken first begins to suspect Becky is cheating when she comes home and immediately throws her panties in the washing machine. She says she had a little accident because she did not get to a ladies room in time. Married eighteen years he really has no reason to suspect anything. But a week later she comes home with a torn blouse. Her excuse is she caught it on a nail at work that a repairman had left in the doorframe to her office. Still he has no real suspicion. However, the following week he sees her stuffing her tights in the washing machine. When he asks what happened Becky tells him she met some of the girls for dinner and when they left she slipped and fell, landing on her rear.

*Well,* Ken thinks, *that's three strikes, she's out.* He begins to wonder who the other guy might be. Maybe her boss or one of the head ad execs at the agency. Maybe some younger guy. It could be someone he knows.

When reality settles in, Ken realizes a divorce will be much too expensive. Becky will get their house and maybe the cottage near the ocean. She will get her car and a good portion of his savings. No, a divorce will not do, but neither can he stay with a cheating wife.

Ken realizes his only course of action is to eliminate his problem. So he begins thinking about how he can do Becky in. His first thought is to take some of the nearly invisible nylon fishing line and tie one end to each side of the top of the stairs. He will do it at night when she is asleep so that in the morning when she goes down for breakfast she will trip and fall down the stairs, maybe break her neck. But if her neck is not broken she might survive and she or someone might find the fishing line. If she does break her neck a police investigation will find where he had tied the ends of the fishing line. He watches enough crime television to know.

Maybe he will cut the brake lines in her car and after the fluid leaks out as she drives from work she will have an accident or the brakes will not work as she tries to slow while coming down a hill. The police will figure it out.

Ken's next choice is arsenic. He reads how slow poisonings can be achieved with arsenic, so her life appears normal while she slowly meets her demise. There will be an autopsy and traces of the poison discovered and the husband will be the prime suspect

Ken's next method of elimination is to back out of the garage and accidentally run over Becky in the driveway. *Nah,* he thinks, *too obvious.*

As he is thinking about all these alternatives the front doorbell rings. He opens the door and two policemen stand there.

*Hell,* he thinks, *they can't arrest me or convict me for what I'm thinking.* The thoughts clear and he asks, "Officers, how can I help you?"

"May we come in?" the sergeant asks."

"Of course," Ken says, "come right in and have a seat on the couch. Are you here to ask for a donation to the Police Charity Ball?"

The sergeant with a serious look worries Ken. "No sir, we are here because ...," he hesitates, "we are here because your wife had a serious accident."

"Accident? Is she okay?"

"Well, she was crossing Lincoln Street and a speeding car went through a red light and struck your wife. I'm afraid she died at the scene."

Ken's mouth opens but no words exited. "Oh m-my G-God," he stutters.

"Is there anything we can do for you?"

"No, no I can't think of a thing. I ... I'm too confused. What do I need to do?"

The sergeant stands up, walks over to Ken and puts his hand on his shoulder, "My suggestion is have a stiff drink and call a friend to stay with you. In the morning we'll send a car over to take you to the morgue so you can identify the body."

Ken nods and leads the police back to the door. *Good idea* he thinks pouring bourbon in a glass. He downs it in two gulps and heads for bed. On the way he smiles.

## When Dreams Come True

I got to bed exhausted from laboring all day refurbishing cables on the George Washington Bridge. It is harrowing being hundreds of feet above the Hudson River working on those cables with only a safety line.

I fall asleep almost instantly and dream I am a knight in a king's court riding a white steed as I rescue a damsel held captive in a tower guarded by a fierce fire breathing dragon that has baked half a dozen rescuers in their armor then devours them while the helpless princess looks on in horror.

I am determined to climb to the parapet and slay the dragon as it naps after a meal of baked knight, but as I climb a rope up the side of the castle my alarm clock rings. My wife makes a sighing noise as she rolls over in her sleep and says, "Have a good day and be careful."

"I will," I say, then kiss her and add, "you are my princess and I will save you from the dragon."

"Silly man," she says with a sleepy smile.

## A Startling Discovery Watching A Moon Of Saturn

Nestor and I are at the observatory looking through the telescope at Titan, one of Saturn's moons.

"It looks like the resorts along the Maine coastline," I say.

"That's silly," Nestor replies, "Titan is nothing more than frozen methane."

"But look at the shoreline, the hotels, the breakwater, the cruise ship off shore," I say.

Nestor looks at me sadly, "It's your imagination, there's nothing there but frozen methane. Perhaps," he concedes, "there might be some liquid methane, but there is no life."

"Not as we know it, but there is life there," I say. "There's a little man standing on the roof of a hotel near the beach waving at us."

## Drag Race

Someone paints a line across the road and two cars pull up side-by-side their wheels behind the line. A girl, a senior in high school, stands between them with a white windbreaker. She looks like Natalie Wood in *Rebel Without A Cause* wearing a skirt and light blue sweater, so proud to be selected for this honor. When the light turns green she jumps up and down waving the jacket. The drivers have one foot on the brakes and one on the gas. The roar is deafening when the spectators cheer as the tires screech at the starting line leaving an acrid smell. The cars enter the dark night while a half mile ahead more spectators wait at a white line painted across the road. The cars barrel toward the finish line. A white jacket waves like a checkered flag for the winner whose prize is glory, bragging rights and a night with the girl at the starting line.

## Fish Story

I do not slept well for three nights, rolling around in my bed like a balloon full of water. Then on the fourth night I dream I am out fishing and catch a flounder. It gives me a bit of a battle until I finally haul it into the motor boat. I manage to get the hook out with little damage, but the fish wriggles out of my hands and flops around the bottom of the boat like a jumping bean. Suddenly it stops flopping and looks up at me.

"Why are you doing this? I was out trying to get dinner for my family and you yank me out of my natural environment and threaten me with death."

I am astonished, but respond, "I'm looking to feed my family too and you seem to be the best candidate for the honor."

The fish flopsd a bit, stops and says, "A dubious honor it is. Do you have children?" It flopsed again and waits for my answer.

"I have two young ones who particularly like fried fish."

Again the fish flops a few times when I say fried fish and then tells me, "I have young ones too they happen to be in a school at the moment, but tonight they will want supper and it won't be there. They'll starve today and tomorrow and then they'll go out looking for a meal and end up being one instead. And what about my wife? She'll have to find another fish."

That makes me think how I will feel if my children are starving and my wife finds someone new.

"You're just playing on my sympathy," I say. "Perhaps everything you say is true. So what should I do, throw you back?"

The fish opens its mouth, it is breathing hard, "I suppose that will be too much to ask, but you could put me in that bucket of water and share some seaweed with me while we discuss this further."

## First Reading

Other poets read for an hour and a half before Hubert's name is finally called. He reads his poem and everyone applauds so he reads a second one about Alzheimer's Disease and they applaud again. Hubert shyly asks if he can read one more and people giggle and heads bob up and down. When Hubert finishes an old lady tells Hubert she loves him and a blonde says she wants to take him home. This will be our first date she tells Hubert who protests that he is married, but she says that is irrelevant. Hubert sees a female police officer about to write him a ticket so he runs out to the car, kisses the cop.

## Bud's Secret

Bud Devlin is not the smartest or best looking guy in high school. He certainly is not the strongest, yet he always has the prettiest girls chasing him. It is not that he is rich, because he is not. He does not play sports or smoke dope or drink alcohol. So when the tenth reunion came along we ask the girls why Bud? None will  say, nor will they reveal Bud's secret at the twentieth, thirtieth or fortieth reunions.

At the fiftieth reunion Dolly DeRoma tells us that Bud is stupid and the girls do not have to pretend to be smart in order to impress. They go out with him because he pays for dinner or a movie, does not talk about anything and always walks them to the door never expecting a kiss.

"We always call him Bud Light," Dolly tells us.

## 1950s Horror Movie

Beautiful blonde, thick lips, skimpy gown, tossing in her sleep seeing the grotesque face of a scarred man limping as he creeps toward her. She wakes, screams – no hope – she faints, he carries her off to a cave in the hills – she begs for freedom, he grunts. Camera moves in for a close up of his gory face. Next scene he eats dinner and we realize it is the blonde he is munching on as he limps off to find another victim. A frozen food commercial follows.

## Are We The Only Ones

I read a magazine article the other day claiming the Milky Way galaxy has 100 billion planets, maybe 200 billion. That made me wonder if we are on the only planet where we go to work every day and deal with rush hour traffic jams.

## Teenage Memories

Fickle they were, young girls, seduced by a car, preferably red. Chosen over personality of youthful folly, swayed by the hum of the engine, roll-and-tuck bench seat and hooked on slicked down hair combed into a DA, selected over a crew cut or whiffle. Liz liked a white T-shirt with a pack of Camels or Chesterfields wrapped in the sleeve. She was attracted by tight black chinos, thrilled by his lips caressing hers, his hand roaming. Her former boyfriend left behind wishing he was old enough to drive.

## Lola

Driving on the turnpike heading home late at night with radio blasting keeping me awake, the Kinks sing Lola as I tap my foot to the music making the car speed up and slow down, with the net cumulative effect of my driving about twenty miles over the speed limit. Soon a blue light flashes behind me with a siren wailing. Pulling over I hear a voice boom out on a loudspeaker, "Turn off the motor and put your hands on the steering wheel." I do as ordered and wait for the police officer to come up to me. It is a female officer saying, "Lower the window." I cannot not because the motor is off. The window is electric, so she signals me to get out of the car, orders me to turn, spread my legs, put my hands on the car. She pats me down, tells me to walk a straight line. She requests I spread my arms, touch my nose, first with the index finger of my right hand, then my left.

"You realize you were exceeding the speed limit by twenty miles per hour."

"Actually officer I didn't. I was tapping my foot to the music," I tell her politely, explaining I was seduced by Lola.

"I see," she said, "you like to dance while driving?"

"No, the music just got to me, it's a great beat."

Grinning she says, "There's a dance down at the high school, follow me, we'll probably have a good time."

## German Shepherd Guards Against The Ghost

The same dog that sticks her head under the bed when there is thunder is prepared to take on the ghost in the bedroom every night at ten. It is inexplicable how it comes each night at the same time, more precise than the scheduled train. One minute before ten the dog rises from the warm rug in the den where I am about to watch the news and slowly makes her way a few feet across the foyer to the bedroom.

Her head and front paws cross into the bedroom, but the rest of her is outside prepared to pull the front end out in a hurry. At exactly ten my brave German Shepherd begins to growl and the hair on the back of her neck stands up. She stares at the upper corner of the bedroom as her growl becomes more throaty, more threatening, a warning she will attack.

Is it the parent of the upstairs couple or the ghost of an Indian or settler who battled over the land? Whatever it is this is her territory to protect unless there is thunder.

## Daily Ritual

Benny's morning consists of lying in bed listening to talk radio. Breakfast, a bowl of cereal and weekdays a clerical job. The apartment is always a mess. He does not own a television. Benny's dinner is another bowl of cereal. At night he again lays in bed with talk radio. Benny does not have much else to do except sleep then repeat the ritual.

## At The Bingo Game He Stands No Chance

Curly enters the bingo parlor hoping to win enough to pay for the bus home. He lost money at the craps table and figures being the youngest person in the room he will have the best hearing and fastest hands to put tokens on numbers. His husky voice will be heard throughout the room when he yells, "Bingo!" But the gray haired octogenarians have the ears of hawks, hands faster than cobras and voices loud enough to be heard one hundred miles away. They are competing for each game prize of twenty-five dollars and the night's grand prize of two hundred and fifty bucks.

Tonight grandma brings home the green.

## Watch Out For The Right Leg

Try to tell her you are sorry you missed a date but she does not want to accept your apology. You try every excuse, broke a leg, fractured a rib, lost an eye, caught the flu, had pneumonia, a temporary case of botulism, was recovering from bubonic plague, ate bad peanuts, caught tongue on an ice cube, tore pants on the streetcar, fell into an open manhole, stampeded by circus elephants, caught scarf in an escalator, rescued a family of eight from their burning home, helped police capture an armed robber, got lost in Philadelphia, kidnapped in Camden, helped deliver a baby in a tunnel and finally, stopped a possible suicide. As you drop to your knees and beg forgiveness all she does is laugh as she raises her right leg and her shoe hits your face.

## Graffiti in the Harvard Coop Men's Room

Written above one of the urinals someone wrote:

*God is dead*
—Nietzsche

Underneath another writing:

*Nietzsche is dead*
—God

## September Morn

Paul Émile Chabas paints her form standing naked washing herself in the pool of water. Not looking at you or me, just dreamily into the fog on the shore. Is her lover there? She exits the pool, wraps in a towel, capitulates to desire. All this in a 10 x 22 masterpiece.

## The Only Man In The Universe

Bob comes home early to tell his wife the bowling team did not show up and finds the bowling team, his friends and neighbors, college roommates, high school buddies and his family gathered in the living room for his surprise fiftieth birthday party. Bob's wife brings out a giant chocolate cake, Leonardo's Pizza s delivers twelve different kinds of pizza and everyone brings a gift. Even Bob's children get him something. There is lots of food and dancing and all the guests are smiling and laughing. As they leave everyone agrees it was a wonderful time. Bob and his wife put the children to sleep, clean the house, go to bed and make love. Afterward, while his wife sleeps, Bob stares out the window at the stars and thinks he is the only man in the universe.

## Belly Laugh

The space ship descends on the 50 yard line in the middle of the Army-Navy football game at Lincoln Financial Field in Philadelphia. Coming down in what appears to be a metallic object about thirty feet high and 15 feet wide. The creature steps out of the space ship yet does not seem to frighten anyone. He, or maybe it, is roughly seven feet high and three or four feet wide. It holds up a hand, or what resembles a hand, perhaps as a sign of peace. The President of the United States sitting in the stands jumps up and imitates the motion. The creature signals the President to come forward. Having a big ego and being brash the President walks out to midfield. He is followed by three Secret Service Agents and two Philadelphia policemen. The President's bleached blonde hair flaps in the wind. His nose is a bit red in the cold and his orange face has darkened. His overcoat is unbuttoned to reveal a white shirt and red tie. His belly protrudes as he walks up to the creature that towers above him. The President signals his body guards to hang back. As the President opens his mouth the creature opens his and like a chameleon a tongue flashes out, grabs the President, pulls and swallows the man who claims to be the smartest and most powerful man on Earth. The body guards scatter, and everyone runs for the exits. The creature stands at midfield with a shaking belly, climbs back into his space ship and takes off.

## High School Reunion Dance

Class reunion dance and there she is as gorgeous as ever doing a slow dance with her husband, a faraway look in the Neptune blue eyes like all those years back. It is the same look as when one of the boys climbs on her in the back seat of a Chevy and then talks about it saying her brains are between her legs and her breasts are lighthouses to guide boys to her. After graduation she goes to college and is not seen again until this night. With our rounded bellies, our hair falling like graying leaves, our gait slowed, our flags mostly at half mast, our vision enhanced we watch her. Her brains may be where we said so long ago, but it gets her the guy who drives a Bentley, gives her diamonds as if they are dimes, worships her as an astronomer does a supernova. She does not see us.

## Book Collector Buried With His Friends

Homer collects books, thousands and places them haphazardly on bookshelves or stacks them on the floor four feet high, even on the kitchen table, in cabinets and under counters. He put books of all sorts on top of dressers, the piano and the couch. The subjects vary. In fact Homer's meagre apartment looks more like a bookstore than living space, yet he only reads a few hoping to become scholarly through osmosis of their contents. He has thousands of books, so when he dies, a coffin is fashioned from them.

## Gourmet Tour

When a space ship lands in the field outside Bedlington, Iowa crowds gather to see what the action is all about or maybe what is piloting the vessel. A few hundred people stare as the entryway to the space vehicle opens and five aliens arrive on Earth and unfurl like a flag spreading over the field covering it like rugs in a living room. Many of the people rush over them to get to the space ships. When nearly a hundred are on them the aliens roll themselves up and get back in the space ship.

## Grammar Ain't What You Think

There is an old joke that goes like this:
A Boston man comes to New York by train and hails a cab. He asks the driver to take him to get scrod.
The cab driver responds, "I've heard it said many different ways but never in the pluperfect subjunctive."

## High School Reunion

High school reunions are like old timer games, most of the players you cannot recognize but you applaud when you hear the name. They are not at all like they were in the old days with hair turning or turned gray and many of them not moving like they did before. They say "You look great!" then later they are sad that you are not what or who you used to be while you wish you are not at the reunion.

## Loneliness

On the Island of Repentance a lone soul seeks forgiveness for love that never was, for lovers scorned, for hearts cracked like ice, for anger in the chest wrapped like a burrito. The soul weeps for those who suffer like lonely bachelors, who serve as prey and whose pain is bleached bones. The lone soul on the Island of Repentance climbs the single palm tree so the world can see the coconut of sorrow ripe for the fall and ready for rescue.

## Photograph

Black & white photo from a Brownie flash camera with white border and scallop edges. She is wearing a white, sleeveless dress with rhinestone cat's eye glasses. Now a glue backed piece of paper is stuck across the face. Yet, I still remember our first kiss.

## After The Beach

Sangria, Ripple, it does not matter much when we are at the beach. We drill a hole in the watermelon, pour the stuff in, shake it up well until it all seeps into the pulp. Bottles discarded, cops are unable to find the source. Red wine + red pulp = no evidence. The more watermelon, the more drunk we get. Couples strewn across the sand like horseshoe crabs washed ashore, kissing, touching, feeling good, forgetting rules.

## First Car

I still remember the Stromberg heads, GlassPaks (aka Hollywood Mufflers) the roar of thunder for the gods. As I rev up an old man down the street shakes his fist and dogs cower, tail between legs. Birds fly away and cats scramble under porches as my car rumbles.

My first car, a '55 Mercury, takes on my friend's '58 Olds and another buddy's '60 Dodge. any car. It does not matter: a Chevy, Ford, anything that dares to go up against my car, my fastest car, my announcement that above all of them I am the greatest, the fastest, the coolest.

## Not Good Enough

Virgil wants to go out with Tara Milton. He longs to date her but she is the most popular girl, her blue eyes constantly sparkling, her blonde hair waving in the air as she leads the cheerleading squad at Longfellow High School.

Virgil is on the football team but he is not the star quarterback or a wide receiver catching touchdown passes. He is a sub and while he can play three or four different positions competently with ease, he is not a recognized hero in the sense that Tom Masters is.

Virgil is, however, the only boy in the school to get perfect scores on the SAT exam and the highest marks in the school. He is accepted to all the Ivy League schools and five other top universities.

The local papers do stories on his above average athletic skills and his remarkable academic achievements.

So that Tuesday when he stops in at Beardsley's Drug Store for a chocolate cream soda he spotsd Tara Milton looking downcast, alone in one of the booths.

"Hey Tara, why so pale and wan?"

"Huh? Oh, I don't know. All the cheerleaders have dates this weekend except me and I feel lonely."

Virgil slips into the booth, sitting across from Tara. "You know I don't have a date this weekend, in fact I rarely have one, so what say we go to the Thai restaurant on Canterbury Boulevard Saturday night?"

"Tara's face brightens. You mean it?"

"Of course, who wouldn't want to go out with you."

"Nobody seems to want to. One of the cheerleaders said the guys are too intimidated to ask me."

"Well I'm not intimidated. In fact I've always wanted to go out with you," Virgil tells her.

"You must have been intimidated too. I imagine it must be hard for you to want to ask me out but are too afraid of rejection. I never would reject you Virgil, you're the smartest boy at Longfellow." Tara's words pour out like tea from a pot. On Saturday night Virgil meetst Tara at her home at 6 p.m.

"What a nice car," Tara says.

"It's an Oldsmobile Cutlass Calais, Quad 4, FE3," Virgil says proudly. "It's the second fastest four cylinder automatic after a Mustang. It can out race most sixes and even some eight-cylinder cars".

As he finishes speaking he stopsd for a red light and a boy from a rival school pulls up in a Chrysler LeBaron convertible. He looks into Virgil's car and says, "Hi honey, what's a gorgeous thing like you doing with him?""

Tara looks away from the boy and at Virgil. The light turns green and the LeBaron speeds off, but there is another red light and Virgil eases to a stop.

"Wanna try that again, "Virgil asks.

"Sure."

The light turnsd green and Virgil hits the gas leaving the LeBaron behind until the third traffic light when it finally catches up.

"Bet you can't do that again," the boy shouts.

"Okay, let's do it, Virgil shouts back as he tapps Tara's thigh and whispers, "Watch this."

Down the street Virgil sees a police car in the Public Works driveway waiting for a speeder. The light changes to green the two cars roar off, but as they cross the intersection Virgil brakes to a stop and the LeBaron, doing 70 mph in a 35 speed zone passes the police car which immediately flips on its lights and pulls the LeBaron over.

He drives by the boy in the LeBaron, who looks at Virgil who lifts his right hand and gives a pinkie salute.

After dinner on the ride home they stop for a red light and incredibly the boy in the LeBaron pulls up.

"Not again, "Virgil says.

"No, no. I just want to know what this means," the boy says raising his right hand, pinkie up.

"Means you ain't good enough for this," Virgil says, showing him the middle finger of his right hand.

## Ghost Town

As a feature writer for Live Ghost Magazine I am often given an assignment in the west because that is where most of the ghosts seem to hang out. On this particular assignment in Nevada I take along my girlfriend Patricia because she is an ace photographer. Patty is a prize winner with a camera and as a girlfriend, so I am thrilled she agrees to accompany me. It means I will have absolute proof if a ghost pops through a wall. It also means I will not have to sleep alone.

As we drive down a dirt road that used to be the main street to Friday, Nevada Patty asks if I know why it has such an unusual name.

"On a Friday in 1887 a bunch of drunk miners find a mother lode of silver that turns into Brookledge Mine. Noah Brookledge started the mine and though he is murdered a year later by the miners who think they should share the claim. They are the same ones who decide that since the vein was discovered on a Friday the town will bear that name. They also decide to keep the name of Brookledge Mine hoping that by honoring the man they killed they will not be suspects. The plan works, but by 1898 the mine is dry and everyone leaves."

"So why is it a ghost town?" Patty asks.

"For one thing people who sleeep in their cars here overnight on the ride between Vegas and Elko report being awakened by ghost howls. Some even say there are apparitions moving in these old buildings."

"Do you believe them?" asks Patty.

"I have never really encountered a ghost, but I write a number of stories based on interviews with those who claim to have seen them."

Patty lights a cigarette, blows on the match and tosses it out the window of the car. "What about those stories that don't have a so-called witness?

I thought a few seconds and tell her, "I describe the town and how scary it is at night. Sometimes I tell about the voices or the howls I hear, or think I hear. I give some history and who I think it might be, a sheriff, an old mayor or hanging judge. Other times I throw in a hanged gunman or a school marm trampled by a herd of cows. Lots of possibilities."

"But no real ghostss," Patty says, disappointed she will not see one.

"Keep that camera of yours handy, I believe one will show."

Stopping in front of the old saloon I hear a piano, Patty says, "Let's go in and see who is playing. Maybe it's the ghost of a piano player."

"Maybe it's not."

"You scared?"

"I don't want to know who is in there, and if it is a ghost I don't want to meet it."

## A Woman You Notice

She is a woman you notice. Reminds me of Claudette Colbert in Cleopatra. Black hair that touch shoulders and short bangs and short nose seemingly pasted on at the last minute for which a million women would pay a bucket of money. Kind of tall with a nice figure in tight jeans. She is, as I say, a woman you notice.

I am telling this story because I worry that someday you will run into her and get taken in. Don't get me wrong, I am neither stupid nor naïve. I usually have luck finding nice women.

I met her at a Halloween party last year. She is dressed like a cat in a black leotard with black stockings. She has cat ears and pencil whiskers on her upper lip.

I am dressed like a nineteen fifties beatnik so I ask what a cat like you doing in a house like this. She responds she is avoiding dogs.

"I'm more wolf than dog. You'd be good as a fox too."

"Why thank you kind sir.."

We dance a bit. I ask if she wants to go for a late snack at a place around the corner.

We date for a few months. Occasionally I stay over when her ex-husband has the kids. Other times she stays at my place and sometimes we go away for the weekend.

.        Finally, one night I say, "You know, you are expensive, especially when I pay a few hundred dollars for a weekend. I always put out the money.   Don't you think you could contribute something?"

"No!" It was emphatic and final. "You want to date and sleep with me you have to entertain me."

It's getting a bit expensive, I respond.

"You say you have a six figure income. My ex-husband and my last boyfriend don't make as much as you do, so it shouldn't be a problem."

"That's not the point," I say. "Most women share expenses, maybe not equally, but they contribute."

"Well I don't, she says.  Frank says ...."  She suddenly stops speaking.

"Who's Frank?" I ask.

She hesitated then says, "A man I met on the bus. I go out with him occasionally. He's much older."

"How occasionally?"

"When you are not available."

"And he stays over at your place?"

"Not when the children are home."

I begin to backout toward the front door. "So you're sleeping with him too? What about diseases and all that?"

"Oh, I protect you both."

I open the front door.

## A Bright Idea

Melinda walks down the street as I come out of my house.
"Hi Melinda," I say, "I didn't know you are pregnant again."
"I'm not," she says, "this is my bulb."
"Bulb, what bulb?" I ask.
"The one the aliens gave me when they kidnapped me," she says matter-of-factly.
"Which aliens?"
"Those blue ones, the ones that look like spoiled egg salad."
"Why a bulb?" I ask.
"So I can see in the dark. All I wanted was a simple 60 or 100 watt job. They gave me this three-way thing."
"Makes sense to me," I say starting the propeller on my head.

## Even The Movie's Happy Ending Made Her Cry

Sarah and I go to a movie about a young man whose mother gets lost and eaten by a cougar while hiking in the mountains The grief stricken young man survives on drugs until he finally tracks down the big cat and shoots it. Once free of his obsession to avenge his mother's death he meets the woman he will love and marry.
Redeemed by love he becomes a psychiatrist and helps others overcome their fears, obsessions or miserable existence.
As we leave the theater, Sarah cries, "That movie is really sad."
"But it ends happily," I say.

## City of Dreams and Desire

Christ stands alone at the top, arms spread as if on the cross,
or in a gesture of welcome to the safe harbor of Rio de Janeiro.
The guidebook, however, says there is danger and to stay in
safe areas and out of slums. It also warns to stay away from
strangers and out of taxis.

At the beach bikinis are more inviting than the Christ of cold
stone statue immobile atop Corocavado.

Zvi A. Sesling

## Buoys On Waves

Her rear bobs like buoys on waves, bobs on waves of cement
with people who rush past like gulls to trash and miss the
beauty of a summer treasure: shorts bobbing like
buoys on waves.

## Should Have But Did Not Know

Hank is invited to Diane's apartment for dinner. She is a few inches taller than he and lives in a nice apartment in a good section of the city. Diane is a junior in college and wants to go out with Hank, also a junior. He refuses. When she asks why, he tells her she is too tall and she asks, "What's height got to do with dating?"

Hank thinks a moment, wants to say *Everything*. Instead just shrugs because he is twenty and does not know how to answer.

## Work In Progress

"Well I will admit he looks a little better," Judy says, his "haircut helps, so do the new clothes and shoes."

"Yeah," Sarah puts in, "it looks like he's been working out too."

Paula adds, "Looks like he's been in a tanning machine too."

Kate says, "Well he is improved but he's still a work in progress".

## Used Cars

I like used cars because they remind me of myself, a bit worn, used and sometimes abused. Parts are replaced as they wear down. The battery occasionally needs a recharge. The engine sometimes needs an overhaul, brakes relined and exterior redone. The used car might last longer and have wonderful stories to tell if it could speak. There is the old man who dies at the wheel and the young couple who make love in the back seat. There is the baby born on the way to the hospital, the drug deals, the drive-by shooting, the drag race, the salesman's route and the housewife's daily trek to school. Finally there are the groans and black smoke of a car wearing out.

## Moth Ball Patrol

They come to the counter, little old ladies wrapped in furs that reek of months under moth ball security. The fur drapes on them like laundry hanging to dry, their faces under an avalanche of makeup. They wear thick, cracking red lipstick and their hair, once blue or orange is now ratty gray like an old bird nest. These old ladies smell like the Union Army. They are someone's mother or grandmother and these little old ladies still make warm chicken soup and matzo balls for those who relish it, oblivious to the smell of moth balls.

## So Cold

It is so cold, in fact, below zero that people wrap themselves like roll ups. It is so cold, shivering birds make branches dance and human breath is like steam from a car exhaust. The butcher leaves meat outside saving electricity. The raccoon stays in its den, the cat curls up indoors. It is so cold, the sun comes up late, the car balks at starting and the day moves in slow motion.

## Simple Things

Wallet full of money, jeans and shirt with sleeves rolled up. Boat shoes, no socks. Boston Braves baseball cap, baseball card of Warren Spahn with that right leg so high it could kick the moon instead of plastic Jesus on the dashboard. Car a hot one on a long straight road with the broken white line like an ellipses. Endless tank of gas and no police to stop a speeding driver. Needle at 100 MPH and bottle of root beer to quench thirst.

## Scramble

Jonas can scramble up a ladder faster than any of the other ten-year-old boys in the neighborhood. One day all the boys decide to climb the big elm tree behind Hogan's garage. Of course the first to scramble up is Jonas. Red, Barry and Steve are right behind. They sit up there and pretend they are lookouts for the calvary. At dinner time they all climb down, except Jonas. He looks down and suddenly gets frightened and will not come down. The other boys yell encouragement then call him a *chicken*. His parents try to talk him down but to no avail. Finally the fire department takes a hook and ladder to get him down. His brother says, "Maybe you'll become a firefighter."
Jonas responds, "No way. Maybe a lumberjack."

## Cardboard Gods

The kids pray for a Ted Williams, Warren Spahn or Willie Mays baseball card. They offer three cards, three pieces of cardboard, for one of the gods. They are gods to these young kids.

## Ashes To Ashes

Robbie walks down the flight of stairs from the bedroom to the kitchen for a small snack, perhaps a banana, or chocolate. Some delicious foreign made chocolate. Chocolate and a shot of bourbon. But he ends up with a whole bar of chocolate and three shots of bourbon. Returning to the bedroom he cannot find his wife, though her walk-around slippers are in front of the recliner and her glasses are on the bed. The window is open. Going downstairs and outside to look around he sees in the backyard a circle where the space ship landed.

## A Surprise Visit

Braxton Standish is depressed even though he is a descendant of Miles Standish and always gainfully employed as a jazz pianist at the Out Of This World Jazz Emporium in San Francisco.

Despite that he is also a moderately successful artist whose paintings regularly sell at the Jupiter Gallery in the same city, he remains despondent. Brax, as he is known to jazz aficionados, never achieves the level of fame to which he feels he is entitled.

One night after he finishes his final set at eleven forty-five he drives to the Golden Gate Bridge where he has achieved fame by playing on an upright piano at the halfway point between San Francisco and Sausalito. At Golden Gate Park he begins walking on the pedestrian walkway in the dense fog he holds on to the railing since he can only see slightly ahead. Getting to what he guesses is the halfway mark he stops and stares down. Not seeing anything he climbs over the railing and jumps.

On the way down Braxton suddenly feels himself stop and his body begins to move upward. In the dense fog into which no one can see is a space ship.

## Gustav's Hypochondria

Gustav is a hypochondriac. This is not in doubt. He has dozens of things he believes wrong such as migraine headaches, sore muscles, three different types of flu, encephalitis, blood disease and warts. Those are only the ones about which he complains. Gustav tells us he has Lupus and insomnia at the same time but who really knows. Why his girlfriend stays with him is something only she knows. As for the rest of us if we want to spend some time with Gustav we just have to put up with his complaints, his continuous need.

## Festival of Lights

Jacob Schnitzel is about seven when it happens. His mother and father invite twelve guests for the last night of Hanukkah. They open the dining table so it can seat the extra people. Putting two overlapping paper tablecloths on the table and then dishes and eating utensils. They place their large menorah with nine candles on the table. When everyone is seated Jacob's mother brings out the potato pancakes, apple sauce and sour cream, cooked green beans and carrots. She lights the *Shamus* and then the rest. An impatient Jacob reaches out for one of the potato pancakes and in doing so knocks over the menorah and all the candles. Almost immediately the paper tablecloth catches fire and in trying to put out the flames one of the guests pushes the paper to the floor. Flames catch the drapes which also go up in flames. Everyone panics except Jacob's father who runs to the kitchen, gets a bucket of water to throw on the drapes. The guests then stomp on the pieces which fall to the floor. After a quick cleanup everyone sits down to a smoky dinner. Everyone except Jacob.

## Louis XVI's Last Thought

Okay so we fight over some silly thing, not unusual for two people used to fighting. I go to the florist and buy a dozen newly guillotined tulips to give her, which she throws on the floor crushing them as if she is doing a Mexican Hat Dance or Flamenco Dance, heels clomping on the linoleum floor. That gets me thinking about Louis XVI's last thoughts as the executioner ties his hands behind his back and places his head in the U-shaped slot. All the while crowds cheer like at a modern day rock concert waiting for the blade to snap his neck in two. The executioner pulls the cord sounding the scrape of metal on metal as the blade whirs its way down. Louis XVI thinks *merde*. The people yell hooray, common people celebrating the joy of liberty. They love the demise of the elite and raise their hands to God. Louis XVI's head is now in a basket while his blood flows and the crimson tide of French royalty soaks the stage and the crowd cheers. Meanwhile in the kitchen she tramples my pride and apology then orders me to clean up the mess. I wonder who cleans up after Louis XVI, who takes the head from the basket and places it back with its royal owner?

## Wallbangers

Oh no, they are at it again. You think the bed slapping the wall is those two next door in the middle of sex. But it is not because he is at the foot of the bed banging the headboard against the wall wanting her between the headboard and the wall.

You wish he has the courtesy not to be so loud or scream at one a.m. You expect her not to be throwing those pots and pans that hit the wall.

But he does. She does. They do.

They have broken up twice before: first he moves and comes back, then she leaves and returns. Maybe this time they will both leave.

## Are You Sure It Works

On the planet Kapora the TBXW Special is the most desired vehicle because of its versatility. In addition to traveling at more than one stribolts per egami it can take to the air with a single push of a button and navigate lakes or oceans with the push of another button.

Bodo comes home and yells to Eifra, "Honey I bought a new TBXW Special. It's guaranteed to drive, fly or take to water. And it is affordable."

"Come, let's go for a ride. We'll try out all three moves," he says to his wife as she stands in the door of their home.

Eifra goes with him in their new vehicle and he tells her as they speed along a highway not yet completed, "You know we've been saving for so many cycles of the sun, this is thrilling."

Eifra is silent.

As they approach the end of the road Bodo realizes he cannot stop the vehicle in time. "Push the green button and we'll fly over the end of the highway."

"Are you sure it works?" Eifra asks as she pushes the green button and TBXW Special lurches forward into space.

"Of course," Bodo says as the engine suddenly stops.

## Bat Boy

In the 1950s Dickie McGregor is the Washington Senators centerfielder and his best friend is third baseman Walter (Stem) Stemcarzyk. The two are inseparable after a baseball game and usually can be found in the same bar downing beers or maybe sipping martinis in the hotel lounge where the team is staying. Stem, a bachelor will pick up a couple of women and he and Dickie will have some entertainment. One evening Stem tells Dickie he has a ticket to the rodeo but cannot go because he has a date and gives the ticket to his friend.

Dickie goes to the rodeo in Virginia, about forty minutes from Washington. After a while he gets bored watching men in cowboy outfits ride bulls and get thrown to the ground. It takes him a bit more than an hour to get back to his suburban home where he sees a car in front of his house. Dickie turns off the motor, reaches into the back seat for his baseball bat and leaves the car, quietly closing the driver side door. In his house he finds his wife with Stem on the couch, her blouse off, his pants down to his knees.

"Some date, you rat," Dickie blurts. Dickie's wife sits up puts her blouse back on and Stem pulls up his pants .

"It ain't what it seems Dickie boy, it ain't what it seems."

"Yeah, so what is it?"

Dickie's wife runs out of the room crying and Stem tries to think of what to say.

"Look, I ... we ...." That was as far as Stem gets as Dickie brings bat from behind his back and with a swing that has hit twenty homeruns strikes Stem squarely on the temple.

Three days later the Senators game is postponed so a funeral can be held. The whole team attends including Dickie McGregor, who gives the eulogy.

## Chili Man Remembers

Chili Man remembers that lunch in the high school cafeteria and the long table with students seated side by side, like in a prison. He remembers he always sits next to a friend.

Some students bring their own lunch, often peanut butter and jelly, but that day Chili Man brings a plate of chili along with desert and soda. He walks with it all on a tray and as he walks behind me with the tray over my head someone says something that causes me to jump up, my head hitting the bottom of the tray that Chili Man carries. It makes the plate of chili on his tray flip over and land on him. He stands there with the chili oozing down over his shirt which, of course, makes every student, even the monitors and some teachers in the cafeteria laugh and point at him. Chili Man begins scooping it off his shirt. His friend Andy laughs and points at him so Chili Man begins taking it off his shirt and patting it on Norman who responds by doing it back to Chili Man. Pretty soon they have a private food fight, that is until Chili Man remembers who causes the chili to land on him. He stops and stares at me, his face now dripping with chili. I could see him glower as he turns toward me.

My feet are already moving when I see the look on his face, eyes narrow, arms reaching out for me. I push a chair over so he has to hurdle or go around it, giving me the seconds I need for a head start.

Oh how I run. Chili Man never has a chance to catch me. Now fifty years later at the high school reunion he said, "I would have killed you if I had caught you."

# A Thought After Two Glasses Of Wine

At the Olympics we creatures dive into water from unappealing heights or torture our bodies to propel through water achieving the fastest time. On a planet somewhere in the great expanse of the universe, do creatures with greater intelligence who live in water dive from unnatural heights to land on piles of dirt, or propel themselves through sand for glory and speed records?

## Rocket Scientist

Hank Brownley cannot believe his good fortune. Here he is at the five star Walt Whitman Restaurant on a blind date with Tina Foran, the most beautiful woman he has ever dated. The only disappointing thing so far is that she knows nothing about sports. Not baseball. Not football. Not basketball or even hockey. She is beautiful and that trumps everything.

"The idea in football is to gain ten yards or more until you get into the opponent's end zone."

"That does not make a lot of sense to me."

" It's not rocket science."

Tina says, "Well, I am a rocket scientist at NASA."

## Revenge In A Foreign Country

Frederick Gruber has recurring nightmares, the first of which involves him missing his plane from London to New York and his best friend taking the flight with Frederick's suitcase and wife.

In the second nightmare Frederick is in Mexico City and again his best friend takes his suitcase and runs off with a prostitute leaving Frederick with just a few pesos and nowhere to live.

On a trip to Azerbaijan Frederick leaves his best friend there to be questioned by the secret police.

## Corner Drunk

Sitting on the corner smelly, disheveled with a whiskey bottle wrapped in a brown paper bag holding a paper cup with three pennies inside. He waits for enough money to buy another cheap bottle before someone steals his money, snatches his dream, takes his life.

## Box 110

Lenny Helm starts as a copy boy at the Washington Reporter-Gazette and is promoted to the sports desk. Today he gets the assignment of his life, a baseball game between the Senators and Yankees.

"Get some interviews in the locker room and then cover fan reaction in the seats," his boss tells him. "Get some good short interviews. I want five or six I can use, that probably means ten to fifteen altogether."

In the locker room first baseman Phil Benson rushes up to him and says, "You Helm?" Not waiting for an answer he continues, "Look I got a big problem that only you can help with. You willing?" Again he does not wait for Lenny to answer. "Good. Look my wife is here today in Box 110, Seat 1."

"Yeah, so what's the big deal?" Lenny asks. "Lots of players bring their wives to a game, especially with the Yankees."

"The problem Helm is that my girlfriend is there too. Box 110, Seat 3. Did not know the wife was coming, gotta pray they don't talk to each other. That's where you come in Helm, want you to go sit in Seat 2 between them and pretend you are my girlfriend's boyfriend. Her name is Marla. My wife is Gloria. Sit between them and don't let them talk to each other. Marla knows you're coming."

Lenny goes to the box and says a quick, "Hi honey," to Marla who responds with a smile. Lenny turns to Gloria and introduces himself. They shake hands and sit back to watch the game.

In the top of the ninth inning the game is tied. The Yankees have two outs and a man on third base.

Gloria says to Lenny and Marla, "It sure is an exciting game."

"Yes and Nicky Primo is up," Marla answers.

"Oh, you're a baseball fan," Gloria says.

"I've been to a few games," Marla answers.

At that moment, as the two women talk, Phil looks up at the box and sees they are chatting. It is also the moment Nicky Primo hits a ground ball that goes through Phil's legs allowing the man at third base to score, forever making Phil Benson Boo-Boo Benson.

## Herbert Never Tells

Herbert likes to invent things. His latest contraption is a large chair in an even larger frame, a giant fan at the back and a clock in the front. There are dials and numbers and other doo-dads that, when the gizmos turn on spin and whistle making clanking noises. Herbert decides he will sit in it and turn it on. It is July 4, 1898 and outside an Independence Day parade is in progress. They are playing patriotic music that fades as Herbert moves the handle to his machine forward.

When he moves the handle to stop the machine Herbert sees strange vehicles that move without horses and whose metallic frames shine in the sunlight. He hears music he has never heard before and clothing on men and women he cannot imagine in his wildest dreams.

He pulls a lever back and the dials spin in reverse until he is back to where he started. It is an exhilarating experience. Climbing into bed Herbert George Wells told himself that when he wakes in the morning he will write his next novel, *The Time Machine*.

## A Quick Easy Way To Learn To Ride A Bicycle

I am six years old in the first grade and my father sits me atop
my first bicycle. He holds the handle bars and the back of the
seat running alongside before pushing and yells, "Hold on,
hold on, don't fall."
Somehow I keep myself upright as I hurtle down a small hill,
off the sidewalk and across the street where I bounce over the
curb into the side of a building. My dad yells "Turn, turn." So
I steer left and he yells, "Pedal, pedal." As I try pushing the
pedals he suddenly yells "Brake, brake!" I don't know how to
brake so I steer toward a fire hydrant and my aim is good. I go
over the handle bars and the fire hydrant then bounce off a
parked car, land on the sidewalk and get scrapes and bruises
like someone gathering wild flowers and my father says, "Next
time will be easier. "

## History of Football

On the first day The Almighty creates a football field with an end zone at each end. When He sees what He has done He thinks, *This is good.* On the second day The Almighty creates goal posts and stadiums for worshippers to attend. On the third day He puts stripes on the field with the number of yards from the end zone. On the fourth day He creates two combative teams and on the fifth day He creates the forward pass. On the sixth day He creates field goals and touchdowns and coaches and referees and televisions to watch the competition between two teams. On the seventh day He sits on a couch, places his feet on an ottoman, invents bowls of popcorn and potato chips, pops open a bottle of beer, burps a few times raises both arms and cheers for every touchdown.

## Dream In A Bottle

He used to share her bed. They met at a party, maybe her cousin introduced them. Forget those details. He tells people she models and he works which angers her. She says modeling is work too, but he scoffs at the notion. He does not love her and they argue incessantly, the subject never really matters, just the sense of fighting. He pays little attention to her and she responds by leaving.

He admits he misses her so he sits outside the entrance to her building with a bottle and his dreams seeking forgiveness and reconciliation. Instead she calls security.

He however, will not leave his post or his bottle.

## Farmer's Wife

It is the first tornado in fifty years and it picks me up and deposits me on a farm in Kansas where the farmer's plump wife greets me with a surprised smile, an apple pie and alfalfa coffee.

Her husband is in the fields and the cows are in the barn, white chickens peck at their feed in the yard and the farmer's wife, Dorothy, keeps smiling and feeding me until I make love to her and she keeps smiling and tells me her husband is coming home so she clicks the heels of her red shoes three times.

## Directions

Lew Odell is dispatched to Paradise, Maine and is told by his manager that a small fishing community needs more lobster traps to meet their monthly quota. Eager to see the Maine seacoast Lew takes in his briefcase, an order pad, two pens and a peanut butter and jelly sandwich. He is told it is a three hour ride and he gets to a fork in the road in just under that time. At the side of the road is a man selling Maine blueberries so Lew stops and asks him, "If I continue straight ahead do I get to Paradise?"

The man looks up and says, "Aye, ya, five miles."

Lew thanks him and in fifteen minutes on the small backroad he is in Paradise. He quickly finds the manager of Lobsters, Inc. and takes an order for sixty new traps.

"Going back to Boston?" the manager asks.

"Why yes."

"Noticed you came in on North Main Street. When you leave here, go thataway, he says pointing to South Main Street. Go about a mile, take a left and it will bring you to the highwy."

Thanking him Lew follows the directions which brings him back to the man selling blueberries. He stops and rolls down his window. "I was here a while back and asked about directions to Paradise. I asked if it was straight down the road and you said yes. It was five miles going north. But it's only a mile and a half going west," Lew says.

"Aye, ya, you only asked if going north would take you to Paradise."

## Her Face Streaked With Tears

In a park in Brussels, Belgium a policewoman cradles the head of a fallen horse in her lap as she looks to someone, anyone, for help. She knows the time has come for the horse's end. The policewoman, hair streaked with sweat, face covered with tears gently strokes the great head of the black horse gently. It is laying on its side covered with a blue police blanket as people watch. Adults divert children's eyes. Police lead their horses away.

## Hit and Run

The words she says are like slapping a wet towel on a bare
behind. It is her way of disposing of men because if she hurts
them enough they will walk away willingly.

It is her mistake once too many times. Someone's brother or
roommate or best friend where she lays down and lets him top
her like sauce on chicken because it does not matter to her and
she thinks, *They are all the same.* He beats her, let her crawl out,
stagger into the street where the hit and run occurs.

## Earrings

She cannot remember when or where she had last wore the earrings. They are not diamond or gold but it is the first gift he gives her. The earrings are what is commonly referred to as huggees. At this moment she is very upset that she has misplaced them. The jewelry box does not hold them, nor does any drawer in her dresser. She checks her winter clothes, summer clothes, even bathing suits. No earrings. Perplexed she decides to change her clothes and put on a different pair of earrings and hopes he will not notice. It is their anniversary and she wants to wear them for him. She selects a pair of black flat shoes, black slacks, a dark red blouse and black jacket. She thinks, *It is almost like I am in mourning for that set of earrings.* She brushes her hair and thinks about putting on fresh makeup and brushing her teeth. She brushes first. Then opens the medicine cabinet for her make up. There on the shelf are the earrings. She almost lets out a whoop of joy, but instead manages a big smile.

## Hominid

Remains have been found of yet another hominid This one about 5.2 million years old reveals a couple of teeth that tell it was more ape than human. Not that it really matters because it did not  have to deal with a morning commute or pollution. Neither did it worry about terrorists, bombs, greenhouse effects, gangs or urban sprawl. It knew nothing of  sexually transmitted diseases, politicians, armies, television, riots, organized religion, schools, drunks, drugs, cholesterol, diets and other modern issues. It had simple problems such as survival.

## Bear Facts

Gary is in the pine tree, as high as he can get when the Park Ranger spots him and yells, "Whatchya doin' up there kiddo?" From his perch nearer to God than he ever thinks he will be Gary shouts back to the Park Ranger, "There was a bear here last night. I had to sleep in the tree."
The Park Ranger asks, "What kind of bear, black or grizzly?"
"Don't know," Gary screams, "it had a long nose, mean teeth and a tail."
Sighing, the Park Ranger says, "It was probably a possum. Sounds like you wasted a night's sleep."

## It Had To Be You

She offers herself, but you say, No. She offers herself and again you say, No. So she leaves. You kick yourself in the mouth. No, you do not stick your foot in, just kick it trying to get to the word Yes. As usual it is too late. She is gone. Alone again, you pour a drink.

## Last Night of the Jitterbug Dance

At midnight ghosts hit the dance floor. Zoot suits flap like awnings and skirts twirl like barber poles. White shoes whirl to resurrected music. The building is doomed. The three second blast brings down the ballroom inside and destroys years of memories. As the dust rises ghosts are finally buried and their memories are soon forgotten, end with the echoes of implosion to the music played by a band long gone. The last night is a blast.

## The Spider & The Fly

The fly has feasted well and now struggles in the web as the spider approaches. Does the fly feel fear? Does the fly or spider think?

## The Dead Speak

Archeologists are legal grave robbers. The dead cannot sleep knowing their souls are being stolen, their bones on display like Playboy bunnies to be ogled as if in a zoo of human remains. Mummies from pyramids, mouths open as if to swear at those who steal their bodies, scream silently. At night when the museum closed and curators are at home plotting new exhibits from China, Japan, Africa or Central America. The Pharaohs speak to each other and one says, "An ice cream would be good about now."

## Lunch In The Park

Some days I eat lunch in the park on an old wooden bench splintered by weather, initials carved decades ago and now spray painted with a territorial design of skate boarding youth. Sitting alone gives me the chance to watch students, politicians and alcoholics pass by as if in a parade for my approval.

Other times it rains and I have to eat at my desk overlooking the park. Today it is raining cats and dogs. I mean literally, Great Danes, Greyhounds, German Shepherds, Poodles, all kinds of Terriers and Spaniels, not to mention miniatures.

Then there are the felines, Persians, Siamese, tabbies, calicos and black cats. It is falling balls of fur, as if Moses had visited a new set of plagues upon us. Tomorrow a promise of toads, lady bugs, earthworms and what else? Behind it all there must be a purpose, perhaps new myths for new religions a thousand years hence. The one who restores order, who gets the cats and dogs to cease their descent upon us all, who in this Third Coming puts a halt to the insect-invertebrate invasion, will be revered in that distant future.

Perhaps that is when this day of feline and canine rain and tomorrow's bug and worm assault will be celebrated as a holy day. It will be the day in which everyone will stop for an hour to recall the pestilential event

So on this day of rain autumn displaces summer, leaves fall from the oak, whose acorn is already buried for spring. Ivy on walls has stopped growing. I used to watch the daily progress, spreading upward and across the brick on the building across the street and think that its goal is sufficient reason to watch.

Then, as I munch peanut butter and jelly on a pumpernickel bagel I think of my friend Max, who can quote the macabre of the world like Nazi atrocities, Stalin's famous victims, American Jewish gangsters and other morbid facts

Max is always trying to get a job. He does not like welfare, but the excuses that he receives from companies are euphemisms for avoiding age discrimination lawsuits. They tell him they need someone more junior but not in age. They do not want to pay what is deserved, they want cost effective hires. It really means they are looking for someone thirty years younger who will take the job for half the salary. Even if they ask for a reference and phone number, they will never call. Max goes home. He checks the Help Wanted ads, as he heads to the next interview, thinking to himself, *If they don't want me, screw them!*

## How To Quit

Ed smokes cigarettes as long as he or anyone can remember. Each of his four wives tell him to quit or he will die. Each marriage ends in divorce The truth is that Ed truly enjoys his four packs of cigarettes each day. He also loves lighting up a bowl of pipe tobacco eight times a day. He inhales everything. Yet he refuses to do other drugs saying it is not healthy.

Ed tries to stop a few times. Once in Hawaii where cigarettes are expensive Ed gets himself down to one smoke after meals and one between each meal. He eventually gets down from five to three cigarettes, but as soon as he returns home he is back to his four packs or more.

Ed goes to a clinic, but it does not help. He tries a hypnotist. No good. Then a psychiatrist and all he gets out of that is that he hates his ex-wives. Finally there is group therapy, but in between the meetings he lights up.

One day at an appointment with his dentist, Dr. Stokes tells him he needs to give up the pipe otherwise he will lose his teeth.

"What about but my lungs?"

Dr. Stokes says, "To be perfectly honest Ed I don't care about your lungs, I'm a dentist, only your teeth are important to me. If you are so concerned about your lungs see a lung specialist."

After he leaves Dr. Stokes' office Ed gets in his car, takes the pipe from the ashtray and stuffs it in the glove compartment. Then he takes the pack of cigarettes in his left hand and throws it out the window of the car. For a couple days it makes no difference but on the weekend he is sweating and shaking, but still refuses to leave the house for fear he will buy cigarettes. On Monday he feels like a different person, free of cigarettes and nicotine.

He eats breakfast sitting on the couch, wondering if any of his wives would care. Should he call with the good news?

## Dirty Water

*Well I love that dirty water*
*Oh, Boston, you're my home*
—The Standells

They have been cleaning the Charles River for umpteen years now. They say you can swim in it, but are dredging for years finding goose poop by the tons. You can see fifty or more geese and goslings swimming at one time. When they eat, they poop.

A few ducks here and there really do not matter, but geese are protected and no one knows why. You cannot use a gun, bow and arrow or sling shot. If you do the goose protection police will get you.

Of course the same folks who protect the geese can be reporting on those who are out there mugging lovers as they stroll. Or they can report the rapist who is dragging some poor girl into the bushes to prove his power and rage. No one calls the people police to rescue any victim who dares walk or jog along the Charles River even in broad daylight.

If you really think it is safe to go swimming in the Charles where the HMS Somerset is anchored on April 18, 1775, think again. Back then it is much wider and swimming probably a fun sport to the colonials and British. It is filled over to build houses. Then sewer systems are added that empty into the venerable waterway. All sorts of sand and dirt and tools are heaved with sewage into the Charles so that two hundred years later it is filthy and polluted. So polluted, in fact, that a song is written about it, so polluted only catfish and bad bacteria survive.

If you go sailing all these years after the British warship patrolled you need a tetanus shot to protect against disease. So now they – whomever they are – say it is safe to swim again but if you cannot drink it, will you swim in it?

## Apple Store Ghost

Waiting for the Apple Store to open Gertrude notices a headless woman in the store. A man in the store walks right through her and Gertrude thinks someone should tell him but they are not open yet.

## Change Is Good

Melvin Lipschitz has always hated his name. Always. One day he resolutely marches to court and submits his papers for a name change. The judge asks why and whether he is sure he wants to do it. Melvin answers in the affirmative to both questions.    A short time later he walks out of the court house with his new name, Barry Lipschitz.

## Counting Sheep

Tonight I am counting sheep because the aspirin does not work nor the acetaminophen. Pills the pharmacist suggests fail as well and mother's old remedy of warm milk leads to the bathroom as do the stiff drink and the beer. The lullaby on the phonograph fails as well. So sheep it is and when I get to 7,530, the number of years some religious sorts say the Earth exists I stop and look out the window at buildings fifty to one hundred years-old then take a shower.

## Nowhere Man

When Murphy O' Daley hears the Beatles recording of *Nowhere Man* he knows where he heard it first. He remembers the time his girlfriend thinks they are lost going from Bar Harbor to Rockland on Maine back roads and Murphy keeps telling her he knows where they are. Now, as he listens to *Nowhere Man*, he knows exactly where he is. He needs only look out the window of the space ship to know that Mars is behind and Jupiter is ahead.

## Doing A Peter Pan

I am walking out of the library and down its stone stairs where at the bottom is a brick sidewalk. I notice a car parked in the "Handicapped Only" parking space with no identifiable placard or license showing the driver or passenger *is* handicapped. As I continue looking I miss a stair and become airborne, putting my hands out as if I am flying. Landing on my knee on the brick sidewalk where I roll over in pain. A sweet looking gray haired woman asks if I am okay and what happened. I explain about the illegally parked car and immediately her face changes. She hurries into the offending car and drives off.

# Cafe

The coffee shop is unusually crowded, mostly women in two's deciding on their futures or reviewing the past. A few men sit with women, except one who catches another man's attention, raises his eyebrows in a question to which the other shakes his head negatively and looks at the woman at the next table who stares eternally at her laptop.

Two older women, gray hair cropped short, smile and talk as if tomorrow is around the corner. They rise and leave together holding hands.

In this cafe instead of paintings or photos there is handwriting on the wall which tells how the coffee is made. The windows let in sunshine so there is heat in the summer encouraging customers to buy cold drinks. In the winter it is cold so customers buy hot drinks.

At one table the two women leave their purses on a table as they go to pick up their coffee.

## Poetry Workshop

It used to be a male thing. You would say, John Ashbery or Thomas Lux will be conducting the workshop or at least be the featured speaker. But now with heavy competition many poetry workshop advertisements show a pretty blonde woman.

## Change Does Not Help

Goldberg knows he has to walk through the Aryan Connection neighborhood. After only one block a dozen members of the group surrounded him.

"You look Jewish."

"No, I'm Irish."

"So you're Catholic?"

"Yes, yes, I am," Goldberg blurts.

"We hate them too," the leader says as they beat him.

## Recall

First it is the bed frame which the letter says can collapse. Then it is the blender blades the postcard says can suddenly break. Next it is the vacuum cleaner that can accidentally dump dirt. Of course the car has a recall because the steering wheel can snap off. Finally the house is a problem because the builder uses asbestos. Now I wait for my recall because of some defect.

## Meeting The Boys

Jimmy has just been hired as a sports writer at the Boston Republican-Gazette. There is a tradition for some of the veteran reporters to take the "rookie" out for dinner and dessert.

In keeping with this tradition the guys take Jimmy to Verona in the North End of Boston and afterward to the Café Napoli. While they are having dessert and coffee in walk seven men, one in front followed by six others, two each in three rows side by side. They all have their hands in the pockets of their camel hair coats and after entering the café they go downstairs.

After a few minutes, the crime reporter Matt, says, "Come with me, I'll take you downstairs to meet the boys." He takes Jimmy downstairs where the men are seated at a table, one at the head the other six, three on each side. The man at the head nods toward Matt and asks, "What can I do for you? "

"Want you to meet our newest sports writer, Jimmy Raymond."

The man at the head of the table nods toward Jimmy and says, "Let me introduce you to the boys." He proceeds to point to each of the seated men and names them. He says his name adding, "If you need anything, feel free to call me."

Jimmy naively thanks the man at the head of the table. Years later he learns who those men really are.

## My Neighbor Has A Boyfriend

My neighbor has a boyfriend who visits several times a week. The neighborhood is curious as to what goes on in her house after dark when there is only one light in the window.

His license number does not help because the state will not reveal any details. Neither will the local police department.

One night the men try to sneak up to the window, but outside prowling skunks and raccoons are tipping over garbage pails in search of food. The neighbors try asking her questions but she never answers them directly, usually bringing up a different topic. They think about calling the car dealer, but there is no identification on the car. The cleaning lady will not provide definitive information.

## Night Riders

Josh lives in a small southern town when he is twelve years old.
He picks up a southern accent quickly and made friends easily
with the boys who live on his street.

His best friend is Howie who lives a few doors down the street.
They play Cadaco All Star Baseball all spring and summer and
in winter the Photo-Electric Football Game. With the
neighborhood boys Josh plays baseball in the warm weather
and touch football when it is cooler.

Josh often eats dinner with Howie's family and vice versa. One
day a classmate, Benji, invites him over to play chess and
Monopoly. In the living room over the mantle Josh sees a large
Nazi flag with a swastika, a German soldier helmet and a
bayonet.

"Wow, Josh exclaims, was your dad in the war?"

"No he belongs to an organization that likes this stuff."

When he comes home Josh tells his parents. They are
mortified. "You're not to play with him anymore."

Without an explanation Josh is confused but tells Benji he
cannot play with him ever again. He begin spending more time
with Howie, playing basketball in the driveway.

At Christmas season every house on the street except Josh's
puts up decorations. A manger here, Santa Claus in a sled there,
lights on almost every house. The other boys ask Josh why his
house is not decorated and he tells them he is Jewish and does
not celebrate Christmas. .

On Christmas Eve a night rider caravan of cars and pickup
trucks pulls up to the front of Josh's home and a dozen or
more men in white sheets climb the five stairs to the front lawn
and pour gasoline on it, then light the gasoline so that it forms
a perfect cross. The men then run back to their vehicles and
drive off. Josh is sure he recognizes Benji's father among them.
A few days after Christmas while they are playing football some
of the boys tell Josh it would be best if he and his family leave

town. Josh tells his parents who say to tell them they will leave at the end of the school year.

The boys tell Josh that their fathers say the end of the school year is acceptable.

## Speaking With God

Bob says if you speak to God you are considered religious. If God speaks to you, you are considered schizophrenic. But what if you do not tell anyone and just have a one on one dialogue?

## Quest For The Perfect Swordfish

It must be grilled with black Xs or turned sideways so as to have crosses. Perhaps, broiled, but either way, not long and thin. Short and thick is the only way. Well done as opposed to juicy with liquids running into squash or baked potatoes. The search goes on at the best restaurants in New York, Boston, Seattle, San Francisco, Paris, London, Rome or just about anywhere. They must not marinate or bake, just simply grill to perfection. The palate vote is the final count. A meal to savor. Forget the vegetables, rolls and coffee. Serve the swordfish well grilled.

## Where Am I

Not in Boston any more, but with palm and eucalyptus trees lining streets and eight lane divided main roads with six lane side streets and a guy on the corner holding a clearance sale sign for five bucks an hour. He keeps pushing the crossing light button manipulating the traffic lights. If a female happens by he tries to engage her in conversation, but she ignores him. A police car stops and the cop tells him to stop pushing the light button and he says, "Yes sir." As soon as the police drive away he pushes the button. Someone yells at him and he raises his middle finger.

## Theory Of Afterlife

Weldon is a firm believer in astronomy texts that tell of stars exploding into supernovae whose "stuff" merges with other exploded stars to form new stars. He says Solzhenitsyn writes the same theory about people. When a person dies, the magnetic force, the aura around the body dissipates, releasing the soul into space. Weldon adds here that human "stuff" mixes with other human "stuff" to form new souls. Weldon believes this gives birth to new people. When someone has a de ja vue moment, when they think they have been somewhere before, or are sure they have been there previously it is because their "stuff" and someone else's are locking in on some past memory of mixed "stuff."

## Nothing

Nothing is the same anymore. We do not wonder about planets, but still wonder if life is out there. Sometimes we ponder how long life will last here. Who was it that says we have a future but no past? Someone else says maybe it is the reverse.

The minister tells his congregation that life elsewhere is bunk and that raccoons are the bandits of night so everyone should pray for redemption all day. The answer, the religious believe is that astronomers find a hole from a previous universe but really ask if it is this the eye of the Almighty?

## Underpants

There was the day Basil goes to visit Steve at his home in the Roxbury section of Bostn.. Steve takes Basil on a nostalgic tour of the old street where both live some sixty years earlier. Everything is exactly as Basil remembers it. The two story red brick house in which Basil lived still has the white columns on the front portico. Only the hedges on the front lawn are gone.

Basil thinks back to the 1950s when Roxbury kids give their fathers nicknames. Mr. Berkowitz who lives next door is called *Undershirt* because on hot days he sits on the front porch in one of those white tank tops. Then there was Mr. Cohen who also lives next door. He is called *Mustache* because he sports one.

Then there is Basil's father who is the only father without a nickname, that is, until the day his son does something that makes Basil's father chase him down the front stairs and out into the street wearing his striped underpants. It seems everyone is outside that late afternoon and all the neighbors laugh. His friends immediately tease Basil about the new nickname *Underpants*.

## What You Think About Angels May Not Be True

One Sunday after church Ralph and his minister discuss angels. Ralph says to Rev. Shortfellow, "When the time comes is anyone really ready for the grim reaper in his black shroud, or is it really a she in a hooded dress with a scythe ready to cut a man's balls off so he will not want to go back among the living. I know there are not seventy- two virgins up there because up there there is no sex. So men have no balls and women no breasts. Angels are neuter because the wings will not support balls or breasts and they need to fly around carrying out their good deeds."

Rev. Shortfellow, looka at Ralph sadly and says, "If sex is all you want, go to hell!"

## Love Triangle

Misery loves Company
Company says she loves Happiness
Happiness and Company slowly dance without Misery

## Wilbur's View

Wilbur ignores his lover Lucinda as she unemotionally eats dinner. Wilbur distances himself from his friends who continue their lives as if he does not exist. Wilbur wants change so he prays, but a tree falls on his house and Wilbur is as displaced as his life.

## Noir

It is at Mack's Bar where she walks in wearing a black leather coat like a Nazi SS commander, her blonde hair hidden by a fedora pulled down over her forehead. She might have just walked out of the screen of a noir film. She asks if anyone will buy her a drink and all the men pull out their wallets to volunteer their eight-fifty an hour, but she picks out just one and downs a whiskey and opens her coat. She is naked and asks the buyer of the drink to walk her home. He is found face down in an alley the next morning with his wallet missing. The police investigate and ask those from the bar what her face looks like.

## Two Weeks In Maine

Harry's father sleeps naked in the conjugal bed while his mother wears knight's armor for protection. Harry wonders if they are even friends anymore. They never go out to the movies or a concert.

His father travels a lot on business, often hundreds of miles and his mother sits home alone sewing, cleaning, doing laundry, playing solitaire. She enjoys solitaire alone because Harry's father always points out her mistakes as he does everything with everybody.

Harry does not know what she does all day when he is in school. He certainly never suspects there might be a day lover while her husband dillies or dallies in some city in an other state.

Once, he recalls his parents separate. He is home with his mother for eight or nine months while his father visits family in California or that is what she tells him. He does not mind because in the summer they go to Maine for two weeks and he frolics on the beach with new friends. One day the motel owner where they stay takes Harry and his mother to Rockland for the lobster festival. Harry has never eaten lobster but he soon becomes enamored of the creature.

When Harry is older he figures out that his father must have been with a mistress those months he was visiting family in California, even while Harry is eating lobster. Harry stops eating lobster because it always brings back thoughts of his father carousing with a woman while he is chowing down. Harry comes to the conclusion that his mother and the motel owner must have gotten it on because she tells Harry he could stay up and watch television while she goes for a cup of coffee in the motel cafeteria.

One day, just before they are to return to Boston, the motel owner tells Harry he is going to cook a special meal for his two favorite guests. He is going to cook chicken and takes Harry to the store where he buys a live chicken. Bringing it to the motel, he takes it out back and chops the head off. Then he makes Harry chase the headless creature until it finally drops dead. The motel owner burns the feathers off leaving an odor Harry will always remember, especially when a dentist drills old fillings in his teeth.

# Rejection

Rejection is a horrible, miserable downer, but only if you let it bother you. Never worry your poem or story is not accepted by a magazine either online or in hard copy. The rejection you receive is probably because your work is not pretentious, obtuse, confusing or vague which is what many magazines now seek.

The simple poem is not in vogue because as soon as it is understood, it is rejected, slapped into an SASE or sent to you as return email. Possibly it is just stuck away in a drawer for six months so it appears (a) to get serious consideration, (b) review by four editors or (c) is a finalist for selection.

You know what the truth is, and while you would love to send a nasty note back to the editor who thinks he or she is the god of poetry or fiction or both, you will not do so because you do not want to burn bridges. You are certain someday they will recognize your immense talent.

## Octogenarian

She comes in showing evidence of countless facelifts and penciled eyebrows wanting Travelers Cheques because she is going to Montreal. Then because it is a long ride she asks the man behind the counter if he will drive her there and back.

He answers, "I think my wife will divorce me. Besides it is against the rules."

## Odor

The man has the odor of a thousand smoked cigars snuffed out and left in the closet to grow putrid. At the counter the sales clerks suffer.

## Vacation

Bernard Feldhaus and his wife Mary argue about vacations. He is permitted one, two-week period each winter, which means she wants to fly to a warm climate but he hates to fly. So it goes back and forth.

"I want to go to the south of France or Spain. Maybe the Greek Islands. What do you think of South America, it's summer there now."

"We could cruise there, you know I hate flying."

"A cruise takes a month, you only have two weeks."

Finally they agree. Mary flies to the south of France, while Bernard books himself on Fantasy Flight's Around The Moon Space Trip.

## A Crazed Dog On Main Street

It is a crazed dog on Main Street that July afternoon in '57.
"Rabies," says Alan.
"Distemper," says Dave, sipping beer.
The sun is high and so is Dave. He heads out the door to confront the dog head on. We all gasp, but Alan throws a beer bottle that hits Dave on the head knocking him down. The police come, shoot the dog. Dave goes to the hospital.

## Gratitude Ignored

Stephen Hawking wrote that he did not believe in God. Perhaps he should have. He lived fifty years longer than anyone else with ALS (Lou Gehrig's Disease).

## The Politician

He is an elected official, earning respect and honor. Then he loses, blames everyone except himself. Takes no responsibility for bad votes, womanizing, insulting constituents and additional transgressions. In a store the sales clerks see a disheveled person in a wrinkled, stained suit and filthy house slippers. He still thinks he is the expert on all things, especially those political. Most people think he is delusional or drunk.

## One Big Hit

If you meet Jason you might think he is well off with a nice house and a swimming pool. He has a fairly new car and big flat screen television to complement the furniture. He has another flat screen television in the bedroom and a few cheap art prints from a thrift store.

Behind this facade is a poor man, money run off with losing horses he bets on at the track and the women he chases. Mostly it is the horses that drain his wallet. He continues hoping for the one big hit.

## If The Truth Be Known

Walter never tells his male friends the truth. He reserves that for the women he dates. It is a wonderful ploy he uses to seduce women he thinks worthy of seducing, which is nearly every woman he knows. He tells women he was adopted as an infant because his parents died in a plane crash and his adoptive parents died of heart attacks. He is ten when they all die and is raised by two cousins, both now dead. He has no relatives except one crazy cousin in a mental institution.

When he finishes his story the woman he is with takes him to the bedroom and says, "Poor boy, let me comfort you."

## Epidural

It takes about a year for Hank to realize involvement with Candy is going nowhere. He begins to look at the relationship, which involves conversation, dinners, a bit of kissing and not much else. Like an epidural Hank feels nothing below the waist and is certain Candy has no stimulation or emotion either.

Hank's friends doubt his sanity because Candy is neither attractive nor shakes the intellectual Richter Scale. These friends cannot understand Hank's attraction to Candy except perhaps his desire to conquer the unconquerable. It is a Quixotic venture at best.

Some of Hank's friends speak to him in friendly tones, others disparage his involvement with Candy. Other friends keep a Benedictine silence on the matter. In the end Hank is unable to decipher whatever secret signals it takes to break Candy's code.

## Professor McTurdee Explains

The professor begins his Friday lecture by stating the end of the world will come in five billion years. He says our sun will expand and burn up the entire solar system thus bringing an end to Earth's multi-billion year history.

Prof. McTurdee tells us cockroaches might survive any apocalypse since they begin as trilobites that blossom into four thousand species. Perhaps, he continues, they will populate Earth five billion years from now when religions, empires, kings, queens, presidents and Shakespeare are no longer memories.

He tells us the little critters will have to nest in whatever they find as there will be no books like *War and Peace* to feed on for weeks. The cockroaches of the future will have long forgotten what it is like to live off human food and waste and will never know bread crumbs or chicken leftovers.

It is possible spiders will survive to this point of astrophysical history feeding off cockroaches. To make his class feel better he says it will all end as the sun continues to expand like a red balloon a child has and as it expands the planets of the solar system will be consumed, burning up and even cockroaches will not survive.

## Creeping Up

It creeps up like a slow fog into San Francisco. Age rolls in first with reading glasses, then full glasses followed by the feet slowing down so while playing softball, maybe in your forties, there is a beautiful slam down the left field line and at first base the head says *GO* but the feet say *NO!*

Next blood pressure is up and there are pills for that. The cholesterol is up so statins are prescribed and that is just before the recommendation for 81 mg aspirin, vitamins, fish oil and more blood pressure meds.

Then people start yelling, but a kind person, perhaps a wife or fellow worker, says what you need are hearing aids, which is confirmed at the hearing specialist's office.      Now everything sounds as it has not been heard in years. Water faucets sound like Niagara Falls, electrical equipment imitates an invasion from outer space, telephones cause a jump from the chair, fire engines and police sirens are harbingers of the world's end.

## Disappearing Act

He comes in wanting to buy some stuff and pays with a check. The clerk asks him to wait for the check to be approved by the manager. When they return to the counter he is gone. The manager says that guy has bounced checks before and does not want to be caught. She reminds staff that the man's picture is on the overhead security cameras.

## Dumpster In Nebraska

There is a dumpster in a Nebraska cornfield in the middle of nowhere. The dumpster is green with six yellow letters painted on its side: D-U-M-P-E-D. In this dumpster are all the dumped people, lovers, wives, husbands, boyfriends, girlfriends, old friends, acquaintances, parents and children. Piled in are egos shrunken to a pinhead, feelings crushed like grapes, emotions burned out like the desert, desire empty as an open can of corn. They are all gray as a clouded sky waiting for sunshine, waiting for a chance to be rescued maybe to be dumped again.

## What Happened To Everybody

Morty drives to Texas to visit his old high school buddy Alvin whom he has not seen in fifteen years. He particularly wonders what has happened to Cynthia his girl friend in his senior year. He manages to track her down through a couple of other high school pals and learns she lives in Oklahoma City.

Morty checks maps and chooses a route through Oklahoma City on his way to Dallas. He gets to Oklahoma City around four in the afternoon, calls information and finds Cynthia's phone number. He knows she has a job and probably will be home later in the evening, so he goes to a local pub and eats a hamburger, fries and root beer, then checks into a motel.

Cynthia answers the telephone, surprised it is Morty on the other end. "Where are you?"

"I'm in Oklahoma City," he says, "had to call and say hi after all these years. I'm on my way to Dallas."

"Why?"

"Going to see Alvin, but I never forget the first girl I, ah, kiss," he says, remembering there was more than kissing that senior year. Beluga, Ohio High School back then is known for seniors engaging in very close contact.

"Ah," she giggles, "I'm a married woman now."

"Pity," Morty says, "But I stopped in Oklahoma City to say hi and ask you about Larry, Davey, Ike and the rest of the group."

"Well there's sadness. Davey had a heart attack last year and died, much too young. Ike was killed in Vietnam and Larry moved to California and I don't know anything else about him. Are you visiting Alvin in Dallas? If so ask him about Sally and Wayne."

"What about them, they broke up senior year, didn't they?"

"Yes, Sally married a man about thirty years her senior and has three kids. Wayne is gay, lives in Florida with some younger guy. When his father died he inherited a lot of money."

Morty laughs, "You know in gym he was always looking at the guys in the showers. We used to kid him about how small he was and he'd get so angry. Freshman year he was the only guy with no pubic hair and that's when we started picking on him and calling him names."

"Yes, I remember you telling me that one night in the back seat of your Chevy."

They both laugh at the memory before Cynthia says, "My husband will be home soon and I haven't even started dinner. Say hi to Alvin for me, he was always a nice guy."

"Too bad," Morty said.

"Too bad what?" Cynthia asks.

"That you're married and he's coming home."

Cynthia hangs up.

## Friend or Foe

There are many people we consider friends, yet we rarely analyze the relationships. Mitchell is a friend who uses friendship so he has someone to listen to his complaints or to gossip. Mitchell is a buddy only when he wants or needs something. Mitchell gambles too much and needs a friend with enough money to loan him or bail him out of debt. Mitchell is a friend who drinks too much and needs someone to drive him home, to be there when he wakes up.

## Old Car

Twenty years he drives that 1977 Datsun B210. Datsun makers never think it can last. Then it dies, the car moldy where water leaks in. Rust all over, the brownish-orange blending with the car's blue. Seats torn, the back seat strewn with books, papers, old clothes. Anyone will say it is a real mess, but he keeps it, refusing to junk it. He keeps driving it until someone runs a red light and the old car is a total wreck. He stands and watches as a tow truck hauls off the Datsun B210 to the car grave yard. His next car is a 1995 Oldsmobile Achieva, moldy where water leaks in, rust blending with blue ....

## Insanity Is Passion

Move in weird patterns, stop at green lights, give the lady who honks the finger and while you are at it, flip one to the boss who does not understand the passion put into the job or how it he drives workers insane trying to make them meet goals, deadlines, commitments and quotas.

No guns necessary to emphasize insanity.
No words needed to prove the passion.
No acts of insanity.

Don't pull your pants down in the conference room.
Don't tear your shirt off.
Don't scream.
Don't cry.
Don't laugh.
No speeches either.

Insanity is passion.

Show them all your passion by quitting. They will call you insane.

## Greatest Magician Disappearing Act

The greatest magician is not the guy who moves an elephant through the Great Wall of China or cuts a beautiful blonde in half. It is also not the kid on TV who does card tricks and it is certainly not the fellow in the black cape and top hat who turns a gorgeous woman into an 800 pound tiger. The greatest magician is T.

Who is T. you ask? Well he is the guy who comes to a party where he knows everyone, slips out without anyone noticing. T. avoids you as if you are a skunk. Call him and he does not pick up the phone. Drop by his house and the doorbell goes unanswered as do the notes you leave. His best act, however, is the disappearing one. The one where after years of friendship he vaporizes like smoke from a chimney.

## It Might Be A Ghost

Patricia calls me in a panic, "The dog is barking," she says.
"Dogs tend to do that," I tell her.
"No, no, you don't understand, Carbo just stands there in the bedroom, looks at the ceiling and growls for a minute or so, then barks. The hair on his neck stands up. I think he sees a ghost," Patricia continues, "I'm convinced Carbo can see the ghost."
"But your house isn't old enough to be haunted," I protest. "A haunted house is usually one or two hundred years-old, or at least a gruesome murder had to happen in it."
"Well there may have been a house here before it was mine. You know how developers are, they tear down perfectly good houses and put up new ones."
"But your house is built where an apple orchard was," I remind Patricia.
She chooses not to hear me and said, "You've got to come over and make sure there's no ghost," she insists.
"How am I supposed to tell if there's a ghost in your bedroom?"
"You'll know, you'll know. I'll leave the porch light on. But I'm already in my pajamas," Patricia says.
"Throw on a raincoat."
I quickly slip on a shirt and pants and rush out of the house to the car. I pass the couple down the hall, a nice older couple, probably in their eighties, who look at me with bewilderment as I rush by in my slippers with no socks.
I drive to Patricia's, dash up the stairs to the front porch. Carbo rushes to meet me, barking from the other side of the front door. I can hear Patricia admonish the dog to stop barking, which he does. Patricia opens the door and says, "Hurry, hurry."
She grabs my arm and pulls me into her bedroom. Sure enough, Carbo beats us there and is staring at the ceiling and growling.

"See," Patricia said pointing, "there's a ghost up there."

I look and listen, but see or hear nothing.

"You're a non-believer," she says with a sneer.

"No, I'm a realist. If there is something up there, it's probably a squirrel or chipmunk crawling around and Carbo can hear it."

"I can't hear any scratching rodents in the walls," Patricia says.

"Dogs can hear what we mere mortal humans cannot."

"Oh, pshaw," she answers disgustedly with a wave of her hand, to dismiss me.

Suddenly I brighten, "Hey isn't tonight that meteor shower?"

"Why yes, let's go in the back yard and watch for a while," Patricia says, seeming to forget the ghost.

We gather up a blanket, a bag of popcorn and go outside. We lie down with the popcorn between us and Carbo at our feet hoping for a little treat.

Patricia is quiet for a few minutes before I say, "There's one, there's another." "It seems funny that Carbo can see a ghost, but not a meteor," I tell her.

## Blessed Are The Children

"Well," Mitheshle says, "our operation is complete with immense success."

"And the children accept our help?" asks Kaskodepta.

Mitheshle looks at his colleague with sad eyes. "Of course. We present ourselves as one of them. We provide the medicine, explain how to infuse their liquids and leave. Children as you know are mistreated in their society, abused, scolded, whipped and overworked. When we present them with the medicine and explain that it will slowly eliminate all who are older they quickly accept it and begin feeding it to adults."

"Yes, of course, but ... "Kaskodepta did not finish his thought. "Being children they do not realize that once all those who are past puberty are gone, they are too young to provide for themselves and will not be able to hunt or farm, let alone reproduce. In a short time all adults will will fall and desiccate. Next the children will slowly disappear either from starvation, fighting among themselves or carnivores will devour them. Blessed are the children".

## A Dime's Worth

The way Jack tells it he is in his first job out of the armed forces, back from Vietnam with two bullet holes still healing. It is late 1960s and he is glad to be out of the military because he cannot stand taking orders or having the enemy pump bullets into him. He searches the Help Wanted pages and lands a job with Carter Omega Advertising & Public Relations. His boss Herbert gives him two small accounts with which he does so well that Herbert gives him Odyssey Computers a $100,000 account from which he makes about ten percent, a lot more than the military.

Anyway, as Jack tells it, Odyssey wants to increase its advertising and public relations budget to one million dollars and invites Carter Omega and five other companies to develop the next level strategy and campaign.

As Jack tells it he is paid fifteen grand a year and his boss drives a forty thousand dollar car with all the bells and whistles. Herbert tells him to draw up an outstanding strategy and campaign. Jack says he does but Herbert does not like it so he creates a new one. They go to the presentation and lose out to Mason, Cork & Villa. Back at the office Herbert calls everyone into his office and screams that they are idiots and should all be fired and singles out Jack by saying "Guys like him like you come a dime a dozen."

As Jack tells it he reaches into his pocket, pulls out a dime which he flips on Herbert's desk and tells him to go buy a dozen.

## Tell Her It Is A Royal Kiss And She Will Love You

He tells her the kiss is royal, her breath purple, rays of sun emitting from the open mouth, her tongue the sword that knights men, her words the army of that seduces, her teeth the gates of paradise and her eyes the guillotine to which all men lose their heads.

## Tale Of The Carrot and Piccolo

Millie lives alone with only her cat Piccolo for company. Since Piccolo is strictly a house cat, he sleeps twenty hours a day and provides little, if any, real companionship for Millie, who likes to lay on her bed and watch television while eating carrots. In fact, Millie eats carrots for breakfast, lunch, supper and even in between. She eats carrots riding the subway, walking in the street and at the supermarket. People stare and children point at the strange sight of an orange lady.

One night in her sleep Millie metamorphoses into a carrot. It is weeks before she is found, a blotch of green mold in the middle of the bed.

Piccolo is nowhere to be found.

## There Is A Protector Out There

Professor Stubbins tells his Astronomy class: "Think of the moon as shield from black stones sent by slingshots from space. It takes a hit for us then smiles to see we are safe."
The class sighs.

## Time Does Not Always Run Out

Louise tells me Stanley is in bad shape. He has a bulging disc
in his neck that causes severe pain. Doctors say he needs an
operation to alleviate it but Stanley says no because what if it
does not help.

Louise tells Stanley what if it does help. Stanley refuses despite
the fact he has trouble with his hands, feet, back and head.

I ask Louise if she is still staying with him and she answers,
"Yes."

I tell her she is a saint for putting up with him. Then I tell her
sister Millie who says," Louise is foolish and should have left
him long ago."

## Hurdy Gurdy Man

Downtown unshaven, wearing baggy pants, rumpled shirt, scruffy shoes, old hat he stands at the corner of Washington and Summer streets with a hurdy gurdy that he winds to make music while a monkey with a hat goes around to the people who watch. The little creature with the long tail holds out the hat. Drop a nickel or dime in the hat monkey chatters, nods, tips his hat then gives money to the hurdy gurdy man. Drop a penny and the monkey gives it to the man and asks for more. How the man can keep winding that machine is a mystery to all who watch.

## High Maintenance

There is a certain lady at a place where Hank works. She is a lady of culture whose father is a diplomat serving in Europe, This lady's upbringing is in the best circles with high couture clothing, and chauffeured limousines. She eats in five-star restaurants and is served by maids and all the rest that goes with privilege. Somehow she gets the notion Hank is wealthy and does her best to let him know of her availability until he tells her he has a small wallet and small car. Then she may as well tell Hank to bug off because she rarely speaks to him again and lets him know through other workers she is seeing a man with a Bentley, a twelve-bedroom house and a summer cottage with private beach on the ocean.

## Friday The 13th

Once I find $200 on this day of bad luck and $20 on another Friday the 13th and still $10 more on a third Friday the 13th so I begin to think Friday the 13th is a lucky day for me. Then one Friday the 13th on the way to work I walk under a ladder, at the top of which is a man working on a roof. "Boy you are going to have a bad day," he yells down.

"Not me, I don't believe all that bunk," and continue to walk. At the intersection I cross the street, and halfway across I look right to assure no cars were coming, but someone on my left is backing up and runs over my foot.

## Dear Friends

I go to my favorite restaurant, favorite not because of the food but because of the free parking. As I walk toward the eatery two women come out the door to their cars.

How I know it is two cars and not one car is because they stop, hug each other and the one in the red coat walks to the right, the one in the black coat goes left.

Ms. Red Coat gets into a black Mercedes Benz and Ms. Black Coat enters a silver Mercedes Benz. They back up without looking and bang into each other breaking taillights and denting metal.

## The Paddle

Bent over, hands on knees, rear end sticking out waiting for the smack, the clap of pain is a shock. Then comes a wince from the sharp light in back of the eyes and determination to not utter a sound or indicate pain. Give no satisfaction to the teacher, to the class, to the one who swung the paddle, do not say *Thank you sir, may I have another please* as in the movie. It is not for the seventh grader to surrender to the pain from a two inch thick piece of wood with a handle.

## Panhandler

I look at every panhandler and think *There but for the grace of God go I* and a quarter dropped to an outstretched hand.

## When He Died

When he died he left the box under the bed holding things he treasured most, the key to a long since junked car, some baseball cards, a blackened rose, a college ring, a picture of his dead brother and two yellowing love letters unsigned which his wife  thought to tear up but then places back in the box under the bed.

## Lester Bildorp Becomes An Orphan

Lester Bildorp is fascinated with magic. When he hears Gelfman The Magician is going to perform at the New Town Theatre he begs his parents to take him. He begs and begs until they cannot stand the begging anymore and agree to take him to see Gelfman The Magician at the New Town Theatre. He wants to see a rabbit pulled from a hat, a lady sawed in half and a handkerchief turn into a dove that flies around the theatre and returns to the magician's hand and back into a handkerchief.

On the special day the family takes a taxi to the theatre, buy tickets for the third row and settle in. Soon Gelfman The Magician appears on stage to applause and cheers. He performs the requisite magic Lester expected, Gelfman pulls a rabbit from his hat, a red handkerchief turns into a dove and back to a handkerchief and he saws the beautiful blonde in half and puts her back together.

Then Gelfman The Magician announces: "Tonight, for the first time anywhere, here in the New Town Theatre I am going to perform magic that has never been attempted anywhere." The audience oohs and ahhs with expectation. They shout, clap and stomp their feet. "I will need one or two volunteers." The theatre goes silent. No one speaks.

Lester looks at his parents and begs them to go up, "You just have to, for me."

Gelfman hears Lester and implores the Bildorp parents to come onstage. He guarantees them the thrill of a lifetime and says their son will be extra proud of them. Lester looks at them with wide pleading eyes. His lips form the word please. So the Bildorps agree and walk up to the stage where Gelfman The Magician stands with arms spread wide

"Ladies and gentlemen," Gelfman announced, "today you are about to see the single most exciting act of magic ever performed live on a stage before an audience of so many people."

With that he opens a large box on the stage and motions the Bildorps to enter. He closes the box and he and his assistant place a large red sheet over it. He recites some incantations. Then he takes one end of the red sheet while his assistant takes the other end and together they remove the sheet.  Gelfman opens the box and shows it is empty.

"But where are my parents?" Lester Bildorp asks.

"Well, I'm not sure," Gelfman The Magician says, "I said I'd make them disappear but I can never figure out how to make them return."

## Everyday

Everyday Kaminiski, not that one, the other one, recites poetry at the corner of 72nd Street and Seventh Avenue shouting castigations of everything political and social.

Each day Kaminiski carries a small book bag with the strap over the shoulder and at precisely noon extracts sheaves of white paper with hand-written poems.

Seditious some say, maybe criminal, while others think they are incantations to aliens from distant planets or worse, signals to an unseen enemy.

At precisely twelve noon he reads his poems for one hour at the top of his voice, shouting in the direction of people leaving stores or just walking on the street.

He stands at the corner of 72nd and Seventh, removes the hand written poems from the book bag, clears his throat, sips water from a plastic bottle and begins reading.

People stop on their way to lunch from work, or to the welfare office to pick up their checks. They listen to the rantings and say he is a madman escaped from the asylum.

One day a man in a gray suit stands and listens for a few minutes then yells that Kaminiski is an anti-government agent trying to recruit them and shoots Kaminski dead.

Now someone stands at the corner of 72nd and Seventh everyday and reads one poem from a blood stained sheet.

## Surprise Ending

Back in high school there was no one uglier than Betty DeMowbry. She was so ugly not a single guy dare ask her on a date for fear her looks are a disease they might catch, not to mention that the boy who might ask Betty out will be socially ostracized by everyone else.

The girls at school avoid her because it might damage their reputations if one of them is seen talking to Betty, let alone appear to be friendly. So it comes as quite a surprise when we begin to notice Betty's belly getting bigger. All the students hold a lottery and the student with the selected number will ask her what is going on. The agreement among all is the person selected will not be ostracized and life will go on for the boy or girl as it always has. He or she can sit with their clique at lunch, continue to date their boyfriend or girlfriend and, of course, remain a cheerleader or on a sports team or chess squad.

All the studentds sit in the high school auditorium where Laura Klembough, captain of the cheerleaders and unanimously the prettiest girl in the school, draws a name from a big barrel they borrow from the Veterans of Foreign Wars, who use it for their weekly raffles. Laura is blindfolded and wears her cheerleader outfit which exposes her long sensuous arms, the right one of which she plunges into the big barrel and pulls out a single slip of white paper. Tony Gordini, the football captain, removes Laura's blindfold takes the piece of paper and walks to the microphone. *Max Highdigger.* Every single head turns to him. Everyone stares, even Tony and Laura. His girlfriend begins to cry so Tony applauds and soon Max is the recipient of a standing ovation. He stands up and waves triumphantly to his classmates, actually happy his name is selected because he wants to hear it first hand from Betty DeMowbry. Everyone knows she is pregnant, it is obvious now. So a pool is started with bets on who did it.

Before Max can approach her we hear she has married the Chemistry teacher Mr. Wingnut.

## What To Do When No One Is Around

Sometimes I leave a message on my answering machine because no one ever calls and it is nice to hear a voice, even if it is my own. Sometimes I read myself a poem or tell myself the baseball scores. Sometimes I invite myself to dinner.

## Web of Deceit

That spider made a major miscalculation. As long as it stays in its web in the corner of the room it is a *live and let live* proposition. It can catch all the flies and silverfish it can eat. However, living things, even arachnids are greedy and when it expands its territory wandering onto my night table I was compelled to drop an old murder story on top of it.

## Dialogue With Mr. Jonson

I am having a dialogue with Mr. Jonson the cat. He meows and I respond, "Do you want food?" He tilts his head a notch to the left I repeat the offer "Want food?" His black fur rises, the green eyes shine like peridots. "Food," I repeat, "Are you hungry?" His tail twitches, followed by another meow. He heads for the kitchen parks himself in front of his dish. "Meow, meow," he repeats. Impatience is not a virtue. He has been a good cat, has not torn up the couch or done his bad anywhere except the litter box. He catches a mouse and begins his serial killing career.

## The Odor Of Women

Sitting in the husband chair at the women's fashion store ladies of different scents pass by. A blonde after a work out or a jog has the odor of sweat. A heavy lady looks at the jewelry display case next to me with the sweet odor of her bath. Another female, elegant and slim, wears an expensive smelling perfume just strong enough for the world to know she can afford it. They are all there for the fashionable styles that suit them, colors that enhance them and odors.

## I Was Happier

Before that television channel shows microscopic pictures of
mites that live in my pillow or the story about bacteria in my
food at restaurants or newspaper articles about soaps that do
more harm than good and a magazine feature story about cops
who sell drugs to kids and all the other hidden disasters that
frighten me so that now I do not sleep well.

## Jonathan Loses His Job

Jonathan loses his job at the Ameriplex Toothpick Company where he is Vice President. He is not sure why he is let go because he is the chief reason they are known worldwide. Then his wife tells him to leave. When he asks where he will go she tells him that is his problem. Whatever money they have she keeps. She also keeps the car. So Jonathan finds himself penniless living on the street and eating in soup kitchens. He soon learns his master's degree in English does not mean anything. But one cold night in a shelter for the homeless Jonathan begins praying to himself but never hears back.

## Hair and Cigarettes

Thirty years ago in New York City Simon looks much as he does today. Maybe his hair is a bit longer and he has a few pounds less flesh because he exercises. It is possible Simon is a starving writer back then. If you look at the picture of Simon thirty years ago he is thin like a tadpole and has enough hair for two people. In every picture he is holds a cigarette in his hand, a burning ember of addiction, a statement of independence and manhood. Hair and cigarettes. Simon does not care much about the hair, often windblown and too long or too short, neither of which matter. He cares about cigarettes, always has a quarter in his pocket to buy a pack. Always one lit.

## Reach Out And Touch Somebody

The guy on the plane has an empty seat between him and the woman seated on the aisle. He stretches out to take all three seats so she reaches out shoving away his legs. He persists so she belts him, shoves him back where he belongs and says to the guy across the aisle, "Take no crap from your neighbor. You really do not have to love thy neighbor especially when he intrudes on your space."

## The Dead Are Dead

MacIntosh cannot sleep because of dreams foretelling his demise. First, his race across the African savannah, his back clawed by lions. Second, in the jungle a boa constrictor latches on to him. Third, as he crosses Fifth Avenue, a cab slams into him.

MacIntosh wakes up thinking about the three scenarios. Later he thinks *I suppose dead is just that, dead.*

## Fountain Of Youth

When the priest knocks on the door a very surprised Harry Goldfarb opens it.

"Mr. Goldfarb?" asks the priest.

"Yes."

"Is this your son?"

Mr. Goldfarb's brow wrinkles, "Yes. What has he done?"

Before the priest can answer, six year-old Joshua says, "I drank water from the fountain."

The priest says, "It was the Holy Water Mr. Goldfarb, we want to make sure he doesn't get sick."

## Beginners Waltz

Mr. Chips never dances, never waltzes until the woman he meets on the mountain maneuvers him to step onto the dance floor. She wears a white gown with elbow length matching gloves and holds a small fan. He is in a tuxedo taking a tentative step, then more, now twirling around the floor with all the others. Music floats like cloud ripples in a big sky. Still the dancers turn and turn into the night with emotions that rise and fall like waves.

## Angel Hair

Ugly Alice Crucknagel is pregnant there is no doubt. What is in doubt is who the father is. Charlie Neppets, the neighborhood's homeliest male is immediately ruled out and my wife, Carla, is nominated to ask her who go her in this predicament. Alice is neither married nor known to be dating since her former husband Pierce Crucknagel moved to California.

Rumors fly until Carla finally approaches Alice on the way to the supermarket and says, "I hear you are pregnant. I want to congratulate you."

"Yes, I am pregnant, "Alice answers glumly,

"And may I ask who is the father?"

"It is an alien," Alice whispers.

"What?"

"It is an alien," Alice repeats.

"What is? "

"The ones who got me pregnant. They kidnapped me and injected me with their sperm so I would produce a child for them since they can't reproduce. Their world is dying because they are sterile, so they are planning to repopulate their world with these hybrids," Alice says patting her tummy.

The two of them stop walking. face each other. They can feel the eyes of a nosy neighbor peering out the window from behind a single slat of Venetian blinds lifted by a single finger. Carla only tells four people what Alice has confessed and in less than hour the whole neighborhood knows.

Three months later Alice gives birth to a boy. Everyone who sees her walk the baby in a carriage acknowledges it is as ugly as its mother and perhaps its father too.

A few of us sit around at lunch at the coffee shop on a Saturday afternoon discussing it when Betsy says, "It has funny stringy white hair, like spaghetti."

"Like angel hair," someone says.

## Hit Man

I sit sipping Tequila with my friend Pascal Pagineau. Pascal says he is hit man.

Over a drink at Sparky's Bar Pascal asks, "You know the dictator in Latin America who is shot between the eyes at his Inauguration?"

I nod yes and he touches his thumb to his chest. "That was me."

"And the TV executive whose car went off the bridge?"

Again I nod and again his thumb touches his chest. Then he thumbs himself twice.

"Gaetano Fabrizio and Jack Doban," he says proudly.

"The Mafia boss and the actor?" I ask in disbelief.

He nods up and down quickly. "Both of 'em, as well as Basil Benson the ex-basketball star who shaved points and Maria Starza the movie star," he adds.

"I can't believe it, I thought Benson just fell off the roof of his buddy's house and Maria Starza overdosed."

"Yes, that's true," he says, "Benson did fall of the roof of his buddy's building, but with some help. As for Miss Starza, too many pills with her drugs. Her downfall is at a very well known restaurant. When she goes to the bathroom, those pills somehow find their way into her drink."

"That's amazing," I say, "you actually knock off all these famous people and never get caught."

He finishes his drink with a large gulp and holds his glass up to the bartender for a refill.

"The famous, the infamous, the not famous and the wannabe famous, he says with a smile. I'm good at what I do so people seek me out to do it. Crime bosses want to eliminate rivals, corporations want to terminate CEOs, husbands want to delete wives. and wives want husbands to disappear and never come home. Once I did both a husband and his wife. Each pay me, so I do them both in."

"You're kidding?"

"No, I'm a professional, I never kid about my work. Not ever. But right now I'm going to a movie, the murder mystery at the Rialto."

## The Old Hometown

Tony is glad to be back in his old hometown, a small Ohio burg where nothing changes and the same buildings are where they always are. The streets look the same and only the people change. Old folks die while the young have grown, living in the same houses with fresh coats of paint and grass brown in the summer heat. There are still plenty of white fences and red fire hydrants still there for a new generation of dogs to sniff.

Most of the cars Tony sees are new and imported, though he wishes he could see some older models. He sees girls who wear shorter skirts and longer hair and feels happy.

Checking the residence lists at the library he finds most of his friends no longer live in town, probably leavet for bigger cities where they lead smaller lives. Only one old friend stays.

Tony has the top down on his convertible and smells the hometown odors that are still there, fresh mowed grass, cakes baking in open windows and hamburgers grilling in backyards.

## Root

We are in the supermarket when I spot a yoga book about parents and children and how they can bond so I open it and find a drawing of a little boy with the various parts of his body labeled – shoulder, solar plexus, while his penis is labeled "root" and I think my penis is no root, though it does have a lot of names like pecker, prick, weenie, short arm, cucumber, zucchini, banana and so forth. There is also cock, dick, flagpole, wonder stick, jack-in-the-box, magic wand, but NOT root. I suffer through a root canal and have to figure out square roots and I root-root-root for the home team, but I never have a root attach to me. My doctor never checks my root and girlfriends never ask, "*How's your root today?*" No, my private parts remain just that, but money still is the root of all evil.

## Ohio Gray

It starts on Todd Lane in Youngstown, Ohio when Mr. Green's roof turns gray. The next day so does the Demoupoulous roof and then the O'Neill's, the Cohen's and so on, until every roof in the city is gray. Houses start turning gray. Soon people and dogs and cats and pigeons are all gray. Next, trees, grass and every car and bus are gray. From Youngstown the gray spreads to Warren, Stubenville, Xenia, Wooster, Cleveland, Dayton and Cincinnati. Finally every living thing in Ohio is gray. Even the state house in Columbus is gray. Local officials, state officials, even federal government agents come to Ohio seeking a solution. There are so many that they resemble ants at a picnic. The investigation goes on for days, weeks and months with no solution. Local officials give up while state officials return to Columbus and federal agents go back back to the CDC in Atlanta and the HHS in Washington, D.C. They are all duly mystified, but glad to be home with their families.

A few days later there is a report  of roofs in Collinsville, Illinois turning gray.

## Smell

The men in the store stare and think she is drop dead gorgeous. The beautiful woman has long yellow hair of the sun, green eyes and smooth skin. She buys everything at the counter. To the sales clerks behind the counter her perfume smells like rancid meat.

## Touchdown Pass

The wide receiver does his best to deceive. Head jerk to the left, hip to the right, bump off the defensive end, turn and fake on the safety. Then man-on-man down field with the cornerback practically snapping at his heels.

He accelerates, and so does his living shadow. He cuts toward the sideline, so does his opponent. Thirty yards behind them the quarterback spots the target, lifts his arm, and with secure grip throws the football like a missile.

Ball spirals forward cutting air as it rises, hurtles toward the target and descends to outstretched arms. Defender also reaching upward and forward with one hand, while tugging the receiver's jersey with the other, hoping a referee does not see the infraction.

Behind the line of scrimmage a charging defender levels the quarterback who lays smothered underneath the weighty bulk of the linebacker. The quarterback cannot see the results of his efforts but the cheering tells him all.

The ball lands in the receiver's arms. Defender fails and his one hand cannot hold the speeding receiver. Defender slips to the ground and receiver races to the end zone, no one close enough to deter him.

The fans on their feet, cheer while the quarterback still on the ground issues a smile of satisfaction. The receiver wiggles a victory dance and flips the football to a nearby referee.

## Here's What Happened

Jack thinks about Nelson, his old friend in the Marines. Jack from Cohasset, Massachusetts and Nelson from Boise, Idaho hit it off as friends in Basic Training at Parris Island. They both like beer and women so when they get weekend leave they go drinking and womanizing.

When Basic Training concludes both are sent to Vietnam, Laos and Cambodia where they carry out their duties in a lethally professional manner.

Back home for many years Jack decides to find Nelson. He checks every internet site he can think of. Then one day he puts Nelson's full name into the computer and there he is! Jack cannot believe it as he reads the documents and thinks *this is not the same Nelson I knew in the Marines.*

The records that come up on his computer show Nelson has a criminal record. He has domestic violence charges against him with two wives, each of whom divorce him. It shows he is a suspect in a hold-up. He is homeless and breaks into a house where he is arrested on a charge of burglary. A kindly judge note Nelson's military service and medals gives him a three month sentence with three years of probation.

At the same time Jack is searching for his friend, Nelson is on a searching for Jack. One day Jack receives an email asking if he is the Jack that Nelson knew in the Marine Corps.

Knowing Nelson's criminal record Jack answers, *Very sorry to inform you I am not the same person you seek but good luck in your quest.*

## Fenton Waldo's Journal

Entry 117: I, Fenton Waldo am alone again. The children set out in a boat to find another home, hopefully they will find living people. Ever since the asteroid shattered the moon, by my estimate probably thirty years ago based on the size of the children. It left pieces of the moon in orbit and other pieces thrust into space. Then the water bearing comet crashed into the Pacific Ocean and as it melted the waters around the world rose to cover the planet. A few people live at the top of tall buildings, but those buildings will rot from the bottom and collapse into the ocean. The true survivors may be those of us who have found a safe cave in the high mountains.

Entry 210: I have lost track of time again. The children have not returned and I pray they find safe haven somewhere. The ocean is maybe two or three hundred yards below this mountain top. By my estimate, Helen died a few years ago. I miss her. I keep scratching time passing on the wall of the cave by marking it with vertical lines. Then I add a horizontal line. Then another. It is so many years, but we – the children, Helen and me created vegetable patches and nets to catch fish, especially the sharks which feed our family.

Entry 269: Ate some kind of fish today. Strange color and shape, but tasty. Ocean has not risen or receded. I suppose no moon means no tides. Alone here is not pleasant but I still live. I go to the mountain top and see only the vast ocean. No other life. No boats. No other life near here yet I am sure the children will succeed in finding a home. It still rains and I catch water to drink. Years ago we figured out how to preserve the vegetables and fish meat. I survive on that.

Entry 334: By my estimate I imagine that another year has ended. Pieces of the moon still shine a bit. My beard and moustache continue growing, but I trim them with the old pocket knife that serves to cut the vegetables and filet the fish. Occasionally I hear voices, but it might be the wind or the water lapping or neither. But I know there are no voices here.

I sometimes think I will go mad, but then I think about Helen and where the children might be. Children? No, they are adults and perhaps they have paddled a great distance or the currents have taken them to a place where others survive. I can only pray for them.

Entry 401: I have not written in a long time. I have not heard from the children and I continue to pray they are still alive and have found friendly people. Maybe Mona has found a partner and I am a grandfather, at least on the way to being one. Luke and Sam? I hope they have someone too. Humanity must continue. I am hopeful the water will recede. It did for Noah, maybe for the rest of us, though this was not a flood from God.

Entry 441: I pray for good fortune. I am hoping someone in a boat comes by. I am hoping the children have found a home. I hope the person or people who found Helen's body floating did not eat her flesh. I keep hoping.

Entry 496: I must write hastily and hope it is legible. With no moon there is nothing to stop an asteroid from hitting us. Today the sky is dark, a giant thing in the sky is approaching, I can see it with my naked eye. It will hit the earth and the planet will shudder and shake. I wonder if anyone will ever read this.

## She Offered Me Her Seat

On the trolley the day I turn forty I suddenly feel eighty because a young lady offers me her seat. She in her twenties, dressed for business carrying a briefcase that makes me think she looks like a lawyer who has just won a court case. I, a bit bedraggled, shirt wrinkled from heat, sports jacket over my arm no briefcase which I left at the office.
I give her the once over, spot the engagement ring shake my head.

## When She Wasn't Looking

"Why would anyone keep the box under the bed," mother yells, "what is in there, anyway?"
That is something I have no intention of telling her and when she is not looking I take the box to the woods, bury it in a deep hole with the hope that some day it will be found like an archeological find and the finder will wonder what sort of person saves these things and why did they bury it.

## The Road Mistaken

According to Google Maps it should be a thirty seven minute ride, but instead the GPS takes me on backroads and side streets so that it ends as a nearly one and one half hour trip. When I get there I realize I know where I am and probably can do the ride on my own.

## The Oscar

I am not nominated and I do not win. My victory speech is written. I tuck it away to read to myself. I thank my director, producer, cameraman, stunt men and co-stars. I acknowledge all the Hollywood beauties who bare a sufficient amount of cleavage.

I remember to thank my cousin Amy for teaching me fake crying, my high school drama teacher for not using me in the senior play, my wife for leaving me for my best friend and my children for recovering from drug addictions. Finally, I thank my parents for abandoning me at birth so that I fight and scrape and pull my way to the top.

I thank all the powers controlling the universe for letting me be up until midnight watching winners.

Zvi A. Sesling

# A Thousand Faces

## I

The crowd begins coming at five, carrying chairs, fold up tables and coolers with dinners of chicken, lamb and vegetarian bean salad appetizers, gazpacho, potato salad, bottled water, iced tea, canned soda and ample wine for the many who like King Kong swat bugs and mosquitoes as if they are bi-planes. By the time the bell clangs to signal the concert, first conducted, ninety-five years earlier in Munich, Germany the moon is like a white eye staring down.

## II

At Tanglewood we sit on the lawn, applause rising with enthusiastic anticipation as the conductor takes the podium. In the shed the audience on its feet and on the lawn we sit in nylon folding chairs while the bugs attack like music critics to take on our long pants and sweatshirts, our hats and socks, all sprayed with bug repellent.

## Early Bird

The early bird gets the worm.
What happens to the early worm?

## Predictable Sci-Fi Horror Movies

There is always a pretty young coed, her blouse torn, shoulder exposed along with a hint of cleavage, hair in disarray, one shoe lost. She runs through the dark, foggy woods looking back over her shoulder. Eyes reinforce terror.

## Attraction

What makes her attractive? Perhaps her smile, opening like petals on a rose.. Maybe her hair, tossed casually and riding the breeze like leaves on bending branches. Then again it can be her wit sharp like a sword, making its point. Or, can it be her quiet dignity or confidence. Perhaps it is that touch of shyness and insecurity in her beauty.

## Road Etiquette

Danny is teaching in Brussels, rents a car for the weekend so he can drive to the North Sea. He needs to go up a narrow street lined on both sides with parked cars in order to get to the main road. A little more than three quarters of the way to the end he sees a Mercedes Benz sedan turn in from the direction Danny is headed. The Mercedes driver honks, then honks again. The driver in the car facing Danny lowers the window and waves for him to back up. Danny waves too. The man gets out of the Mercedes and Danny exits his Ford Fiesta. The man says something in French, so Danny asks if he speaks English.

"Oui," the Frenchman says.

"Well your car is a really big Mercedes and mine is a little rented Fiesta," says Danny.

"Oui," says the Frenchman.

"Well, I'm more than three quarters of the way to the end and you just turned in," Danny continues.

"Oui," says the Frenchman.

An angry Danny says, "Well if you don't back up I'm taking this little rented Fiesta and ramming into your quarter million dollar Mercedes Benz, and since you turned in, guess who'll be blamed."

## Never Pick A Fight With Big Luke

The mayor and Big Luke chat outside a bar on Main Street. Big Luke, who is eighty-two years-old tells the mayor that during World War II Joe Louis, the heavyweight champion of the world, raised money for the USO by traveling the country and boxed three rounds with five different men. Any man who could last three rounds received one hundred dollars, a princely sum in the 1940s.

Big Luke says, "Joe Louis fought five guys in Worcester and I was the only one to last three rounds. He never even knocked me down."

The mayor asks, "Wow, Luke, why didn't you continue fighting?"

"I was drafted and when I got out of the service I met Mae and she didn't want me boxing no more so I opened a gym for young kids."

As they speak a young man in his twenties comes out of the bar and pushes Luke who is blocking the doorway. "You shouldn't stand there."

Luke says, "Sorry."

"If you weren't an old man I'd belt you," says the young man says making a fist.

Insulted, Luke responds, "You can try kid."

With his fist still balled up he swings at Luke who steps aside and lands his own fist on the younger man's jaw knocking him out cold.

Someone calls the police who quickly arrive and ask the mayor, "What happened sir."

The mayor points to the young man still unconscious and lying on the sidewalk, "The kid took a swing at Big Luke here and Luke decked him. He'll have a hell of time explaining being ko'd by an old man."

## Manure

Herschel, high school graduate at eighteen, decides to live for one year on an Israeli kibbutz. He ends up at Beit Hashita where his work assignment is in chicken coops. He is provided with a wheelbarrow and shovel and told to fill the wheelbarrow then take it to a truck and dump it. Despite wearing a bandana to cover his nose and mouth Herschel contracts a sinus infection. After a week of antibiotics and a stay in the infirmary he is sent back to the coop where he informs the supervisor he will not work with the dry manure again. The supervisor says he understands, gives Herschel a pair of knee high boots, a shovel and wheelbarrow and sends him to the wet manure to fill the wheelbarrow that he carts out to the back and dumps to dry out.

For years Herschel calls the kibbutz Beit Ha Shit.

## Behind A Cemetery

Mack Browning lives behind a cemetery. At night coyotes howl but neighbors say it is ghosts wailing, the ones headed down and the ones who get no visitors to remember them. The pain of being forgotten is too great for ghosts whose corporeal being is slowly melting beneath sod so they rise to wail their misfortune, to tell the world they want to be remembered. Mack does not believe any of it and turns on the football game. The Red Devils are playing the Blue Devils.

## Always All About Him

Weldon never calls anyone, they always have to call him. He never leaves his house to visit others. He insists on always cooking. Weldon never goes in a swimming pool that is not his. He is the one who always has to choose the restaurant when he goes out to eat with friends and it is always Italian food. And if you want to listen to music he never likes your choice because only his is worthy of listening.

Everyone knows Weldon is narcissistic. He leads a lonely life.

## Harley Was Afraid Of The Werewolf

There are always men waiting for the full moon. As the moon rises Harley sees a man grow hair that covers his body like a wolf. The man becomes a werewolf seeking prey, human blood for sustenance. It is a nightmare of fiction, but for Harley it is reality. He watches the blood sucker feast and sees the night beast whose shadow makes him run.

## Neighbors

Leon and Iris sit in their living room with Phillip and Joan. Phillip tries to convince their hosts that their son Irving should go to Russia with them.

Philip says the boy will lead a good life, become a Communist leader and restore the homeland's glory. But Leon and Iris resist and will not let their son be taken away.

Days later FBI agents knock on Leon and Iris' door and ask for Philip and Joan. Leon points to the other door on the third floor and agents redirect themselves, knocking on Philip and Joan's door. When Philip opens it they arrest him and Iris as Communist agents.

Meanwhile another agent asks Leon if he knows the people on the first floor and Leon says yes he knows Mr. Caravelli. The agent tells him Mr. Caravelli was found floating face down in the river yestday. Leon is shocked, asks what happened. The agent says the Mafia got him.

When all the agents leave Mr. Caravelli's apartment, Leon whispers to Iris they are going to move.

## Advantage To Being A Senior

On a warm, sunny Tuesday Sam drives down Commonwealth Avenue enjoying the sights of the Boston University coeds walking to class in shorts and t-shirts. At a red light a man probably in his thirties jumps out of his car and pounds on Sam's window.

Calmly, Sam exits his car standing eye to eye with the man and asks, "What's wrong?"

The man screams, "What's wrong? You cut me off back there you stupid son of a bitch and nearly scared the life out of me."

Sam apologizes, "Oh, I am sorry, I guess I didn't see you when I changed lanes."

The man yells some more, "You guess! If you weren't an old man I'd punch you out." He makes a fist to show he means it.

Sam says, "You know it's a felony in Massachusetts to hit someone over sixty and I'm seventy-two."

"Really?" The young man drops his hand to his side.

"Yes," Sam says, "but it's only a misdemeanor for me."

Zvi A. Sesling

## Someone Must Like Her

Someone must like her. Look at the streaks of blonde and brown hair falling over bare shoulders. Then there is the cleavage undulating like vanilla custard as she moves slowly to the music. Nothing sexy about her at all when you realize she is out there by herself, eyes closed, her dancing partner an image jumping among neurons and synapses. Maybe she sees blonde tips on spiked hair. Perhaps it is three buttons on the shirt open to reveal the waxed chest and gold chain. Maybe he has Travolta moves in his repertoire. Her lips are slightly parted as if he says something wonderful to her, perhaps lies about her beauty, calls her sultry or maybe even touches her in a way that pleases. Now her arms above her head descend to her sides as eyes open and mouth closes. The smile fades like old flowers because her virtual lover vaporizes like steam in a cappuccino machine. The music stops as she walks back toward her seat.

## Homeless In Paradise

My name is Gilbert, Gilbert Merrick. You probably heard of me. I was the guy who made the plans for the fifty-one million dollar heist on Wall Street. Jeb Willard, Frankie Proust and I pulled it off three years ago walking out of the largest brokerage house with three suitcases, each loaded with seventeen mil in greenbacks. We decided to hide out separately. Then came the story about the first space ships to reach the Kepler Seven. Seven planets orbiting around a brown dwarf sun. I watch the news and learn that each planet has life bringing the total to more than five hundred in our galaxy. Anyway Kepler 1, the nearest to the dwarf star is warm all the time with warm oceans and trees that resemble palm trees on Earth. Kepler 2 has only spring and autumn, a pleasant place. The news reports Kepler 3 is like the South Seas with nice weather in summer and much rain the winter. Kepler 4 is a bit cooler, more like a year round autumn on Earth, Kepler 5 produces a late autumn and light winter. Kepler 6 has mostly mild winters great for winter sports.. Kepler 7 is like Earth's Siberia, extreme cold, heavy snow conditions for which we humans are barely fit. I pick a planet sure I have more than enough to pay for the flight. Of course, once there I realize greenbacks are worthless.

## Childhood Memories

Ten years old and the kids in the neighborhood think I am nuts trading a Ted Williams baseball card for Warren Spahn even up. Even nuttier for swapping three other cards for Earl Torgeson.

When my neighborhood friends wear Confederate caps I wear a Union soldier cap in our civil war battles.

In the street I run a few races in my P.F. Canvas Shoes and eat my Hoodsie with a wooden spoon and suck popsicles in hot weather. I read ten cent small hardcover Tarzan novels and nickel Classic Comics. And, of course, there is always my American Flyer electric train for rainy days.

Four years later I am wearing tee shirts and jeans, riding a Schwinn bike and gulping down burgers, fries and milk shakes. I have some awful teachers in a school with ramps instead of stairs. When no one is watching my friends and I roll trash barrels down and cheer when they smash into the wall on the floor below.

Once caught we get detention after school in a study hall thick with uninterested students. We go to the first rock concert in town and the first kiss is done outside the high school dance. Soon I am kissing someone else. And soon after that ....

## Go West

Listen to Horace Greeley, get in a car go west. Get on that super highway, push the pedal down to 65 or 70 mph. Only stop for gas, food, bathroom. Save money by sleeping in a motel parking lot where there is a surveillance camera. Keep driving to anywhere west of the Mississippi River. Forget politics.

## Knock In The Night

A knock in the night and I wonder if it is her returning from where ... a lover ... a bar. She has been somewhere since the moon rises over the city and the dog howls its protest. Her side of the bed is abandoned and is now refrigerator cold matching her affection. Can the knock in the night be her returning or the police? Is the knock in the night in my head?

## Chicken Dinner

I am in kindergarten, my teacher speaks German and Spanish
my parents speak German and Russian and my aunt speaks
German and Spanish. I speak only German. The maid only
knows Spanish. I understand a little Spanish and my aunt says
to the maid, who doubles as cook. We will have chicken for
dinner. The maid waves her hand for me to follow her to the
backyard signaling with her hands says, "Catch the chicken,"
so I chase the white one around the yard with the energy of a
five year-old while the maid yells for me to corner it. When I
finally grab it, it pecks at me, tries for the eyes, settles for the
hand. I drop it. Like Chicken Little it is off again seeking
freedom. The maid grabs the bird by the neck, tucks it under
her arm, then gives the head a twist and before the maid, the
chicken or I know its condition she lays the fowl's neck on a
wood block, produces an ax and severs the head with a
competent blow. I learn then that chickens run around with
their heads cut off and fifty years later I figure out politicians
do that too.

## Chicken Dinner II

The cook chops off its head tells me to grab the chicken, but I am frozen in time and space so the cook catches it, hands it to me and shows me how to pluck the feathers. He burns the stubs off, a smell I will recall years later in a dentist's chair when he cleans out a cavity, the smell filling my nose with bad memories, especially those of dinner on a night when roast chicken is served on a plate in front of me and I am told *Eat!*

## Pulling A Tooth

Brady takes his wife to the dental clinic where she is about to have her lower left molar extracted. He drives to the door of the dentist's office, drops her off, says he will be in as soon as he parks the car. As he enters the office a young, attractive receptionist asks which dentist he is to see. Brady says he is waiting for his wife who is having her tooth pulled, so the receptionist points to some chairs and tells him to have a seat. Brady picks out one he thinks looks comfortable, grabs a magazine from the rack and becomes engrossed in a story about a movie star who has two wives and three mistresses and wants to be a candidate for congress from a district that has many movie stars. As he turns the page a dental assistant announces Brady's wife is ready to leave. She is sitting waiting for him to pay the bill. Brady looks with genuine surprise and says, "She is not my wife!"

"Of course she is. This is June Davis."

"It's not. I know my wife, we've been married thirty years. This is not the woman I married. My wife is five-three with black hair and blue eyes. This woman is ..."

The dental assistant interrupts him and says, She is five-three with black hair and blue eyes."

Brady says, "She is wearing a black, Estrella winter coat and furry black boots."

The dental assistant points to the woman in the black coat and furry black boots without saying a word.

The woman looking up to Brady says, "What's wrong dear? Pay the bill and let's go home. This tooth extraction is very uncomfortable and the gauze has to come out in fifteen minutes."

"B-but I d-don't know who you are. You are not my wife. You look a little like her, but you are not her," Brady says.

"Of course I am sweetheart," the woman says, "I'm just minus one tooth."

## Da Da

I am moving to another house and trying to figure out how to transport my thousand books. The mover tells me it will cost several hundred dollars based on weight, the number of boxes, the time it will take to pack and carry them out to the moving van. Then add in transport costs followed by carrying them into my new residence. He is generous telling me I can save money by packing and unpacking them myself. After due consideration I elect to hold a sidewalk sale and proceed to set up a few folding tables on which I placed bestsellers, fiction and self-help books, stuff I know moves fast, while the other books I place in boxes, spine up so the title can be read. Others are placed carefully on the stairs of my apartment building. When the books on the table sell, I move those from the stairs and boxes to the tables. It was going pretty well until a little man came along wearing a wrinkled black suit with thin white stripes, a not ironed shirt open at the collar. He also wears a black hat. He looks through the boxes solemnly and suddenly jerks a book out of one of the boxes,

"Lev," he says in a reverent whisper. "Lev," he repeats and strokes the book as if it is a beautiful woman and leafs through the pages as if he undressing her. "Lev, Lev," he continues to murmur.

"Who's Lev?" I ask.

He points to the cover, of *War and Peace* by Leo Tolstoy.

"That's Leo Tolstoy," I say.

"Da, da, Lev," He responds.

"Your Lev is Leo?" I ask.

"Da, da," he continues answering in Russian.

"It's a hardcover book," I say, "that's a dollar," and hold up a dollar bill.

"Da, da," he says and hands me a quarter.

I take it, sympathetic toward someone who seems a half-mad Russian. Smiling, he shuffles off down the street with *War and*

*Peace* under his arm. In the distance I hear cannons and the 1812 Overture.

## Caveman, Pharaoh, Immortality

When they retire the baseball player's number it is declared he is the greatest in team history. People flock by the thousands to honor him. Music plays on the loudspeaker and speeches are made. Someone says he is immortal now.

Immortal? Cavemen's bones are excavated from land that once flourish with fauna and flora but now the bones reside in a cave where they sleep at night away from carnivorous animals that reverse hunter and hunted.

Not even Egyptian pharaohs are immortal. Their blackened remains empty of their organs are plied from the earth, x-ray tested, studied and finally displayed in foreign lands of which pharaohs could never dream. The mummies are now in place in a modern Cairo they could never imagine.

Now a baseball player who hit many home runs and won games by the dozens, but who cannot not field that well nor speak like a scholar but can spot a fastball and time his swing to send the ball over the fence for a homer bringing a cheering crowd to its collective feet is called immortal.

Yes, he wielded his club to feed his family as the caveman did and his cave is called a dugout. He eats up opposing pitchers enough to have his number placed on a wall in the Hall of Fame. However, will he be remembered in two thousand or ten thousand years? Or will he be like those who were not the greatest?

## Some Days Are Just Plain Bad

The boss yells at you when you try to help someone. A coworker yells at you when you try to assist. A customer yells at you because you are not fast enough. You are behind the counter all day. You look in the mirror and yell at yourself, *What am I doing here?*

## Book Store

Claxton owns a bookstore where the books are piled high on wooden shelves. People enter and walk around worshipping the authors thinking books are bibles telling truths or possibly reveal secrets or recipes. All the books in Claxton's store are stacked like towers of words thick with fiction, history, many oversized like egos.

## Bury Them Quickly

The Dead Go Fast And Life Goes On
—Kenneth Koch

## Bedroom Ghost

Perhaps it is a bit of undigested meat as Dickens suggests. Or it might be just plain old imagination at work. When I awake in the middle of the night there it is, a dark hulk or ghost, maybe the grim reaper or a dead priest in his cassock. It is there, a round faceless head with body and arms, a shroud that floats out of the bedroom.

## Fast Learner

Clara learns fast. When Seamus meets her she is virgin. In one night he teaches her three tricks and after a week she is better than any escort Seamus hires. Clara also learnq to cook his favorite dish, take care of his dog, clean his apartment, clean his car, change the oil and assure the tire pressure is correct. She learns it all in just one lesson and Seamus begins thinking about teaching her blackjack, so he does. After a single go around in which he has set up six imaginary players plus Clara as a seventh Seamus feels she is ready for the big time, a casino not far from his home.

On their first night at Universal Casino she wins two thousand dollars. The next night three thousand more and the casino management requests she leave. The two of them drive back home happy as a pair of camels at an oasis. They stop at an exclusive restaurant in town, where he eats a filet mignon and she downs a prime rib. They each have two rounds of Glenlivet Scotch then go home and make love twice.

In the morning he leaves for work and she says, "I'll tidy up before I leave." Clara does the laundry and while putting away his underpants finds another cellphone. Knowing Seamus' propensity for using simple words, Clara easily figures out the password since she is a fast learner and discovers he is having affairs with three other women.

Clara is not a woman to be cheated on. She goes to her uncle, a government agent.

"I need help Uncle Fred, my boyfriend is cheating on me."

"And you want to eliminate your rival ?"

"No I want to eliminate my boyfriend."

"I can't do that, he's not an enemy of the state," Uncle Fred tells her.

"Oh, I wouldn't ask that of you. Just give me a weapon and show me how to use it. I'm a fast learner."

Uncle Fred went tgoes o his closet emerging two minutes later with a pistol. "This is a special handgun. You push this button and a red laser light goes on. Point the laser at the target and pull the trigger. But first release the safety," Fred says pushing a button on the side of the gun. He then points the laser at a glass on his desk and pulls the trigger. The glass shatters. " Now you try."

Clara takes the gun aims at a picture of her father on the wall and puts a bullet through his heart. She smiles.

"You really hate your father too," Uncle Fred says.

"He killed my mother."

"She was a spy for the Russians," he answers.

"He killed her," Clara said. "Gotta go" She kisses her uncle on the cheek and leaves..

On the drive she recite the last line of a poem, "Red sky at night, sailor's delight." Then adds, "Red light on his head, Seamus is dead."

## Final Deal

Brian, Greg, Andy and Joe are longtime friends and losers. Each has been arrested for theft, DUI and assault and battery. Each spends time behind bars. Now thirty years old they all enjoy beer, usually a half dozen or more per sitting. Every Thursday they meet at Wolfie's Pub for a few rounds and to commiserate about the miseries of their their lives.

As they sit there on this Thursday night, the last before Daylight Savings Time ends Briane says, "I've had it with this life. I'm ready to go out big time."

"What's big time?" Andy asks.

Brian answers him quickly, "What's big time? Well, Andy old pal, big time is taking out people on the way out."

Greg laughs. "So you're gonna commit the ultimate crime and die doing it, huh?"

"You gonna kill the cops?" Andy is incredulous.

"Nah, I got a better plan," Brian snorts. "I'm gonna see how many people I can take out before they get me."

"Not a bad idea, "Greg says. "We should bet on which of us gets more and the winner takes the money."

"Ain't gonna be no winner because they'll get you both," Andy says but agrees to make it three for the road.

The three of them make a pact to collect weapons, ammunition and bullet proof vests. They will bring whatever they can get and in one month, on a Saturday night they will each select a target and go do their jobs.

When the time comes. There are four assault rifles, four automatic pistols, four Bowie knives and many rounds of ammunition for the rifles and pistols.

Brian says he will take the Emerald Theatre where a few hundred people will be watching a play. There are actors, the orchestra and ushers to snuff out.

Greg picks a movie theater noting there are a couple hundred people and ushers at the popular flick.

Andy says he is going to a high school football game. "Players, cheerleaders and fans for me to get."
Brian change his mind and says  he likes the idea of a shopping mall where he will get the guards first, then the shoppers and store clerks.
They wish each other luck and leave.

## Down The Road From The Mansion

Further down the road is a farm where he grew up, where sheep graze softly in a large field, horses roam the meadow and cows lie on the hillside after a morning milking. The dog barks at anything that moves and chickens cluck defiance at those who steal eggs. Goats bump heads, the sweet smell of drying hay comes in with the morning breeze. Day means work, night means sleep. The barn is the office.

## Hollywood Gunfight

Bob has always wanted to be a reporter, starting in the second grade when he faithfully listens to *Front Page Farrell* on the radio. When he goes to high school Bob joins the staff of his high school newspaper. That is where he meets Darla Stratton. For four years they work together.

One day Darla comes running in excited and sweating and says, "You won't believe this. Steve McQueen is going to be in a rodeo here."

"Wait," Bob says, "he's the star of *Wanted: Dead or Alive!*

"Right, and I have an interview with him," Darla says panting.

"O my gosh, I love that show. Let me go with you."

Darla agrees so the two of them go to the rodeo. After the performance a guard leads them to McQueen's dressing room. Bob asks if the appearance on *The Restless Gun* with John Payne is a trial for his current starring role and McQueen answers in the affirmative. Bob asks what was the funniest thing that had ever happened to him.

"Well," McQueen says, "we are at a party at Dean Martin's house and a few of us had been in westerns and got into a discussion of who is the fastest draw. Well, Peter Lawford said he is. So did Sammy Davis, Jr., Joey Bishop, James Garner and me.

"So, Dean suggests we have a fast draw contest on the front porch and nickname it the OK Corral. He has a couple of pistols that fire red gel capsules that break when hitting something like a body. Of course they are harmless so we put on white smocks and proceed to have a fast draw contest.

"Dean easily beats Joey Bishop and Garner beats Peter Lawford. Sammy beats me to everyone's surprise, including mine. In the next round Dean beats Garner and then has to face off with Sammy. Lawford counts to three and they draw and Dean beats Sammy, who falls to the floor face up and arms spread as if he is crucified.

"Well it seems at that moment a police car drives by and hears the shots and the cops rush up to the screened in front porch. They barrel in, guns drawn, and tell everybody not to move. We put our hands in the air, except Sammy who is still spread out on the floor, eyes open as if he is dead.

"Dean says to the cops, 'We're only using blanks and having a fast draw competition.' Then looking toward Sammy says, 'Come on Sammy get up.' Sammy doesn't move. Dean repeats his command Sammy lies there perfectly still.

"The cops tell Dean to drop the gun which he does at the same time telling Sammy to stop fooling around and get up, but Sammy continues play dead.

"The cops then tell everyone, the famous and their wives to stand against the screen enclosing the porch. As everyone lines up Sammy suddenly jumps up. He scares the daylights out of the cops and one fires his gun and the bullet the lodges in the ceiling."

# Home Town

For his vacation Warren decides he will travel to his hometown. He remembers his address was 210 Lausche Street, the street named after Ohio's former governor and U.S. Senator who died years earlier. The house is on the corner of Lausche and Toledo and he looks forward to seeing it again.

But now as he drives on Toledo and approaches the corner where he lived he sees the house is gone. Nothing remains but an empty lot and he realizes he is at Toledo and Pitt and has another block to go.

Parking the car in front of the house with peeling paint he takes out his camera for pictures of the old place. There are only a few houses left on the street and as he points the camera to number 210 a man comes rushing out waving a pistol in Warren's face offering free advice, "Get outta here now!"

Warren decides he will take the man's advice. He puts the camera in the back and gets back into the driver's seat. As he starts the motor a little boy, no older than ten comes to the window and asks if Warren wants to buy a plastic bag with crack for $5. Warren shakes his head no and drives to the next corner where he stops for a red light. A girl he takes to be fifteen offers herself for a C-note.

Warren takes off through the red light and thinks this is not the city of his youth, this is the present and the reality is poverty, death, fire and drugs.

## The Neighbor And The Oak Tree

The branches of the oak tree in Edgar's yard grow over the fence providing shade and leaves to rake. When a blue jay lands heavily, a shower of snow comes down. Tom, the neighbor, and his son build a snowman while his dog barks.

This spring when Edgar knows Tom is not at home he pulls out the ladder no one  sees him use in years. He brings out a saw which Tom never imagines he Edgar knows how to use and begins the back and forth rhythmic motion until all the branches on his side of the fence are gone and with a smile of satisfaction puts the saw and ladder away and goes out to eat.

Cutting those branches off is like severing an arm and the tree begins to bleed until there is blood in Edgar's yard, pools and puddles of blood as the great tree cries washing the blood into the ground causing last autumn's acorns to sprout all over his lawn so Edgar cannot cut them down fast enough and for each one he cuts, two more come up until his yard looks like Medusa's head and no one can look at the yard or visit him for fear of turning to wood.

## Do Not Flush Paper Towels Or Foreign Objects

Harry reads the sign in the unisex bathroom: *Do Not Flush Paper Towels or Foreign Objects.*

Harry wonders what exactly is a *foreign object*. Perhaps a moon rock brought to Earth by an astronaut or a Martian stone blasted here a million years ago by a cataclysm on the red planet. It might be something from another country, a Swedish meatball, French pastry, Haitian voodoo doll or Chinese bamboo stick. Perhaps none of the above. Then Harry realizes they must mean anything that is not toilet paper. He thinks for a moment, takes off his shoes and socks. The socks are *Made In America* so he throws the socks in the toilet.

## One Small Step For Mankind

It is the moment Zagdorp waits for, a final descent in the flying saucer on to the planet. He and his three hundred space patrol comrades along with their superior weaponry will conquer the planet. He knows they will win, he feels it in his one inch body. The space ship touches down on the sand at Daytona Beach. He sees the sun, the blue sky and the foaming green ocean slapping the beach. Then suddenly everything goes dark as Johnny Meachum's five year-old foot stomps it dead. "That's the end ugly crab," Johnny yells.

## What We Can Hope For

In 1962 the Washington American League baseball team is known as the Senators, while the Los Angeles American League team is the Angels. It is the year Jimmy Piersall is traded from the Senators to the Angels, prompting one sports wag to utter, "Too bad politicians can't be like Jimmy Piersall, a Senator at the beginning of the year and an Angel at the end."

# ABOUT THE AUTHOR

Zvi A. Sesling, Poet Laureate Emeritus of Brookline, MA (2017-2020) has published flash fiction and poetry in numerous magazines both in print and online in the United States, Great Britain, Ireland, France, Cyprus, New Zealand, Australia, India, Canada and Israel. He was awarded First Prize in the Reuben Rose International Poetry Competition. He was selected to read his poetry at New England/Pen "Discovery" by the late Boston Poet Laureate Sam Cornish. His poetry was selected for the Spring Rain Poetry Festival on Cyprus and his Hay (na) ku poetry is part of a display at the San Francisco Library. In addition, he has a Hay (na) ku, two poems and four flash fiction stories in Stanford University's *Life in Quarantine* project. Sesling was twice a featured reader in the Jewish Poetry Festival in Brookline, MA and is a regular reviewer for the *Boston Small Press and Poetry Scene*. Sesling is Editor of *10By10 Flash Fiction Stories* and *Muddy River Poetry Review*. He has been a featured reader in various venues in the Boston area, San Diego, the Massachusetts Poetry Festival and the Boston National Poetry Festival. He has also read on local radio and cable television programs. He is author of four books of poetry, *War Zones, The Lynching of Leo Frank, Fire Tongue* and *King of the Jungle* and and three chapbooks, *Simple Game, Baseball Poetry; Love Poems from Hell* and *Across Stones of Bad Dreams*. He is the author of the recently published flash fiction chapbook *Wheels*. Sesling taught at Suffolk University, Emerson College and Boston University. He lives in Brookline, MA with his wife Susan J. Dechter.